TRUCE AT NUEVIANT

BOILING POINT

"Assemble the men, but be ready for trouble," Wehrmacht Sergeant Franz Weselmann cautioned.

The words were hardly out of his mouth when suddenly there was a high pitched woman's scream that came from the house where the nuns were quartered. The two missing SS men were standing near the front door of the house. Gerickman's staff car was parked alongside on the road.

"The nuns!" Weselmann shouted, sprinting for the house.

Otto Gerickman exited the front door, buttoning the front of his black tunic. A look of satisfaction was etched on his freshly scratched face. The three men, unaware of Weselmann's approach, had found something amusing as they stood in front of the house.

Uncontrollable anger swelled up in Weselmann as thoughts raced through his mind of Sister Monique and what this SS officer had done to her. He was losing all rational control and he didn't care.

Otto Gerickman, starting to head for his staff car, saw the rage and anger in Weselmann's eyes. He had time to say, "This is none of—," before Weselmann's fist slammed into the Nazi's gut, knocking him to a knee.

The SS officer regained his balance in time to receive a crushing blow to his face that slammed him backwards into the door forcing it open. Inside were the two nuns, one was lifeless on the floor and the other was trying to cover her semi nude body with the remains of her habit.

Gerickman rose to his feet, blood pouring from a broken nose.

"How dare you strike a German officer!" Gerickman shouted, fumbling to draw his Luger from its holster . . . .

TRUCE AT NUEVIANT

RON NOWAK

iUniverse, Inc.
Bloomington

Truce at Nueviant

iUniverse books may be ordered through booksellers or by contacting:

iUniverse
1663 Liberty Drive
Bloomington, IN 47403
www.iuniverse.com
1-800-Authors (1-800-288-4677)

ISBN: 978-1-4620-4298-2 (sc)
ISBN: 978-1-4620-4300-2 (hc)
ISBN: 978-1-4620-4299-9 (ebk)

Printed in the United States of America

iUniverse rev. date: 08/17/2011

To my greatest love
my wife Gale

Chapter 1

The German army was bruised but not beaten in October of 1944; the borders of the Third Reich shrank with each passing day as units of Major General George S. Patton's Third Army closed in on the Rhine River. In a small stand of trees, a unit of panzer grenadiers surrounded their sergeant. They were part of Hauptmann Kurt Hauser's 3rd Company, 119th Panzer Grenadier Regiment of the 25th Panzer Grenadier Division. Their company had been assigned as a rearguard while the rest of the regiment retreated to a new defensive line. The seven men had been separated from the rest of company after the Americans broke through their lines.

Twenty-eight-year-old Sergeant Franz Weselmann had fought in Poland, France, and Russia, and his men looked to him to get them out of the ever closing pocket. He rubbed his chin while studying his sector map, his blond hair peeking out from under his helmet. The remaining six members of his squad waited for an answer.

They were all that remained of 2nd Platoon. Many lay scattered in a dozen fields in the French countryside. Some were caught in the open by Allied fighter-bombers who strafed and bombed them into oblivion. Some died in quick firefights with Patton's men, and the rest were taken prisoner. Weselmann hoped that the men who survived their captivity would help to rebuild Germany after the war. He erased thoughts of lost comrades and got back to his main objective: think of a way to get his squad back to friendly territory.

"Looks like the only way out is northeast. A couple kilometers from here is a small dirt road we can take. I imagine the Americans have all the main roads cut off," Weselmann said, his concern overshadowed by the confidence of his men in his leadership. "It's rough terrain but good cover. We should be able to avoid any enemy patrols. How much ammunition do we have?" After each man replied, a quick inventory revealed a little more than sixty rounds of rifle ammunition, less than forty-five rounds of submachine gun ammunition and three grenades.

"We can fight our way through the entire American army with that much ammunition," Corporal Hans Vopel retorted. "Instead of fighting in France, let's just invade Britain and then America. We'll capture Churchill and Roosevelt and end the war." Vopel's comments brought a smile to the faces of Weselmann's men.

"We'll leave Roosevelt and Churchill alone for now and concentrate on getting back to our unit," Weselmann replied. "Would you be so kind as to scout ahead for us, Corporal Vopel," Weselmann requested with a smile.

"Yes, Sergeant Weselmann!" Vopel replied, snapping a sharp salute.

"We move out in three minutes."

After picking up his helmet and backpack, Vopel started heading northeast. As he passed Weselmann, the jolly corporal from Munich smiled, "Don't worry Franz," he softly said. "We'll get the lads back to 3rd Company." In peacetime he was a baker's assistant now the squad's lead scout and Weselmann's closest friend.

One by one, the remaining men moved past the ever alert Weselmann, crunching the newly fallen leaves under their boots.

Private Fritz Stempel was a Bavarian clock maker from Augsburg, a graying veteran of World War I, called up as a replacement. He always reminded Weselmann of his own grandfather. It was no wonder that the squad nicknamed him Grandpa.

Private Karl Baake was a carpenter from Nuremberg who was the best rifle shot in the company. Once several Russian machine guns had the platoon pinned down for thirty minutes. After crawling into an excellent firing position, Baake calmly checked the sights on his Mauser rifle for 350 yards. With seven well aimed shots, he methodically silenced the Russian crews.

Lance corporal Peter Rotter was a pig farmer from Biberach, who at six foot four inches and 250 pounds had no equal in hand to hand combat. Along with Weselmann and Vopel, he was one of the old hands, original members of the squad. The three had been together since the Polish campaign in 1939.

Privates Ernest Bunzel and Franz Piontek, the youngest members of Weselmann's unit, had just been conscripted from school in Nuremburg. Both were only sixteen, and Weselmann hoped they would see their seventeenth birthdays. They joined 3rd Company as replacements, for men lost on the Russian front, when the regiment was transferred to France.

Weselmann waited until they moved ten yards in front of him before joining the column as the rearguard.

The woods were thick and the pace was slow, but there was no chance of Allied planes spotting them. They followed a deer path, not much wider than three feet, through the woods. Weselmann thought it is a beautiful forest. It reminded him of the Bavarian countryside. The leaves that remained in the trees were turning from green to shades of brown and tan. It's a shame that the war would soon tear apart this relative calm they now enjoyed. A combination of the early afternoon sun and the humidity of the woods began to soak their uniforms with sweat.

They had walked for about an hour when the woods turned into a clearing. Vopel spotted something. He slowly raised his hand to signal the others. As Weselmann moved up, he noticed at the edge of the clearing there was the dirt road leading to a small village.

He studied the village through his binoculars, hunting for any out of the ordinary detail. The dirt road ran through the village disappearing into the forest heading east. A small hilltop, behind an old church, overlooked the village to the south. To the north were multiple houses and shops, ringed in by heavy woods. To the southwest were the remains of several houses, in various degrees of disrepair. It was obvious, that the village had seen better days. There was no sign of any life in the village except behind the old church, in what looked like the local cemetery.

"What do you think?" Vopel asked.

"Looks peaceful enough, but so did that small hamlet near Demansk in 43," Weselmann replied. An inexperienced officer cost Weselmann a lot of comrades that day.

"I remember Lieutenant Voss' big ambush. Decided to use the village as a trap, only problem the Russians were already dug in the town. Walked into the town just before all hell broke loose. Got himself killed and made half of 2nd Platoon casualties."

"Let's assume the village is occupied. Take Peter and Karl and circle around to the left to that high ground behind the church. From there you should be able to spot any movement in the village. I'll take the rest and slowly advance up the road. Any sign of trouble, fire a shot."

"Franz, don't you think we should bypass this village and move on? The Americans could be only a few kilometers back," Vopel asked.

"I'd like to, but our canteens are dry and our rations are gone. Take your men and move out." Weselmann's serious look was replaced with a smile. "Any sign of trouble fire a shot and get back here. Don't be a hero and try to earn another medal," he said, pointing to the Iron Cross on Vopel's tunic.

"Don't need anymore. Good looks and what I already have attract the young ladies."

Vopel tapped Rotter and Baake on the back. Both followed him into the woods on the left side of the road.

Weselmann waited until he no longer could see any of Vopel's group. He motioned the remaining members of his unit to start down the road.

"Spread out and be ready to take cover."

Step by step they moved closer to the village and were soon at the edge of the first house. Weselmann motioned Private Bunzel to check out the first house on the left and Private Piontek the first one on the right. Each man kicked in the front door with rifles ready and returned shaking their heads. One by one, each house or shop was searched but they found no signs of life. All that remained was the old stone church at the opposite end of the village.

Weselmann could see Corporal Vopel and his two men on the hill behind the church. He signaled them to check the rear of the church while he and the rest prepared to enter the front doors of the church.

"Piontek and Bunzel, come with me. Grandpa, stay here and watch the street," Weselmann ordered. He waited until his men were in position to cover him, then he crashed his shoulder into the left hand door of the church and came face to face with a young nun.

"Oh," a soft scream came from her throat. "How can I help you, Monsieur?" she asked, quickly regaining her composure. Even in her traditional nun's black gown and white cap, he could tell she was an attractive woman in her mid 20's. Around her waist was a knotted prayer rope.

Weselmann quickly removed his helmet, revealing his matted blond hair and fair features. His piercing blue eyes were highlighted by a flushed red face.

"Excuse me, Sister. We did not know who was in the church."

Piontek and Bunzel entered the church behind their sergeant.

"I'll check out the rest of the church. See if Corporal Vopel needs you."

"Yes, Sergeant," they said in unison, exiting the church.

"Are there any other people in the village?" Weselmann asked.

"Only Sister Genevieve and I remain. The villagers fled the coming battle of your army and the Americans. We have been hearing the sounds of the heavy guns getting closer every day."

"I know, Sister. We mean you no harm. We merely stopped in your village to look for food and water. All we want to do is avoid a fight with the Americans and get back to our lines."

Vopel entered the church reporting, "Grandpa and Peter are watching the road for any enemy patrols, and there is a fresh water spring behind the church. The village is deserted except for an elderly nun working in a small garden out back."

"That is Sister Genevieve, and I am Sister Monique. We have some bread and cheese, which we will share with you and your men. And you are welcome to fill your canteens from the spring

5

your friend discovered." There was something about this German sergeant that she liked. He didn't have the arrogant tone in his voice that previous German visitors displayed.

"Thank you, Sister. I am Sergeant Weselmann and this is Corporal Vopel. We'll fill our canteens and be on our way."

"Hans, have the men fill their canteens," he said, tossing his empty canteen to Vopel. "It could be a long time before we reach another spring or brook.

We move out in ten minutes."

As Weselmann walked with the young nun, he noticed how well the church would make a natural fort if attacked by the Americans. The walls were made of cut stones possibly a foot thick, able to withstand any weapon short of an anti-tank gun. There was a small vestibule just inside the two heavy oak entrance doors. The vestibule led to the sanctuary with two rows of pews leading to a modest altar with a tabernacle and two golden candlesticks. On the left, a staircase climbed into the church steeple; on the right a door leading to either storage or living quarters. A life sized cross with the image of Jesus, overlooking the sanctuary, hung on the east wall of the building. Around the sanctuary were various statues of saints, each one with a collection of candles for prayer requests. A row of four chest high windows on either side of the church could work well for rifle pits. He quickly dismissed any thoughts of fighting in this village with only six men.

After reaching the front of the church, they both genuflected at the first pew.

"Are you a Catholic, Sergeant?"

"Yes I am."

"Your French is quite good. Where did you learn to speak our language?"

"Before the war, I was at university teaching French and English. I know that if I survive this war I will go back to teaching. I hope that this is the last war my future students experience."

He let his mind wander back to his days of teaching before the war. It was good to talk with someone other than the men under his command, and he was beginning to enjoy the conversation.

"But Sister, why did you and Sister Genevieve not leave the village with the rest of the people? This will not be a safe place if our troops and the Americans fight here."

They strolled to the back of the church to view the old nun weeding her garden, ignoring Weselmann's men as they filled their canteens.

"I could not leave sister here by herself, and she will not leave her garden. She has tended her garden since she became a nun here in Nueviant. She loves her garden the way parents love and nurture their children."

As they spoke, they saw Private Piontek drop his pack down on several plants in the garden. The old nun rose to her feet moving as fast as she could to the young soldier. She raised the gardening tool in her hand in menacing way, showering Piontek in a flurry of French that did not sound pleasant.

Weselmann was both amused and irritated by the scene, "Piontek, pick up your pack and get out of her garden."

"Yes, Sergeant," Piontek exclaimed, moving quickly from the upset nun. Sister Genevieve chased him until she was sure he was not coming back to her garden.

Sister Monique chuckled, "You see how sister can be if you bother her garden."

"I could use Sister Genevieve in my own unit. She could put the Allies to flight with her trowel," Weselmann replied.

Sister Monique turned and smiled at the handsome sergeant who returned the smile. "You don't seem to hate us as much as your countrymen. Usually we encounter only stares when we enter a village."

Sister Monique replied, "To God there is no difference between German and Frenchman, and since I will soon take my vows I must love my friends and my enemies equally."

"You said take your vows?"

"Yes, I'm a novice nun. I have three months left in my training."

Her demeanor changed as she continued, "When France surrendered to your army, the Vichy government decided to support Hitler. When the Americans invaded French North Africa, my husband was killed in the fighting. Six months later, I decided to become a nun."

The smile disappeared from his face. "I'm sorry to hear of the loss of your husband, Sister."

Weselmann glanced at his watch. "I have enjoyed our visit, but we must keep moving towards our lines. Goodbye, Sister."

"Goodbye, Sergeant," she softly replied.

There were still several hours of daylight to continue their desire to reach friendly units. He did not want to leave. He wanted to stay and continue this conversation, but he had to get his men home. The more he talked with Sister Monique, the more he looked at her as a woman instead of a novice nun. He thought of her soft, brown eyes and infectious smile but quickly dismissed such thoughts. *We are in the middle of a war possibly already cut off from our regiment, and you are thinking of a young woman who is almost a nun.*

He walked out of the church, replacing his helmet. He barked orders at Vopel, "Does everyone have a full canteen? We are moving out!"

They all nodded to the affirmative.

Vopel sensed that something wasn't quite right. He asked Weselmann, "Franz, what's the problem?"

Before he could answer, Sister Monique ran out towards them with a basket of bread and cheese.

"Sergeant, here is the food I promised you."

Weselmann's tone and demeanor immediately softened as the young novice tried to give the basket of food to the sergeant.

"No, Sister. You and Sister Genevieve might need this food later."

"No, we have more than enough and your men look hungry. Please take the food."

Vopel jumped into the conversation, "Sister on behalf of 3rd Company, I thank you."

Sister Monique smiled warmly as she handed the basket to the corporal. As Vopel began to pass out the food to the rest of the soldiers, he looked over his shoulder and realized what was bothering his friend. Weselmann's eyes told the story as he talked to Sister Monique.

"Oh, Franz," Vopel softly chuckled.

After a few more words with Sister Monique, Weselmann turned to the task of leaving the village.

"Corporal Vopel, you're our eyes and ears. Scout twenty yards ahead of us."

Just as Weselmann raised his hand to signal the unit to move out, the faint sound of many vehicles rumbled in the distance. A cloud of dust was rising near the road at the west end of the village.

"Sister Monique, get Sister Genevieve into the church basement!" Weselmann shouted.

Satisfied the nuns were heading into the church, he turned his attention to the defense of the village.

"Sergeant, do you think it's the Americans?" Bunzel asked.

"It might be them or it could be some of our units trying to get to Strasbourg. But if they are coming this way, the main road must already be blocked."

"Hans, take Piontek and cover us from the church steeple. Peter and Grandpa, set up in the first house. Karl and Bunzel, in the house with the yellow awning. No one open fire unless I do. Maybe they will pass through. Let's move."

The six panzer grenadiers scrambled to their positions while Weselmann entered the church to find Sister Monique waiting in the vestibule.

"Sister, please get in the church basement and stay there until the shooting is over."

The last thing he wanted was for her to be hurt or killed if it came to a fight.

"Are you going to fight? Wouldn't it be wiser to surrender, and then no one would be hurt," she replied, hoping she could change his mind.

"Sister, I do not have time to discuss this now. Please get in the basement now," Weselmann insisted angrily.

Weselmann peered out of the slightly opened door to get a view of the road. Looking over his shoulder, he noticed that she had left

9

for the basement. He hated being cross with her but it was for her own good.

The first vehicle burst out of the woods, a motorcycle with a black-clad rider, followed by a variety of other vehicles. Weselmann's first thoughts were a unit to tag along with until they could find their own company.

Weselmann sighed deeply when he saw their pennants, "Gestapo."

Chapter 2

The swastika decorated black BMW staff car sped down the paved road, the afternoon sun glaring off the hood ornament. In its wake was a detachment of SS Gestapo, fleeing the advancing American Army. The collection of trucks, staff cars, and half-tracks were having a hard time keeping up with the leader. Slightly ahead of the column were two motorcycles, complete with a heavily armed passenger riding in the sidecar.

Sitting in the back seat of the open command car was the officer in charge of this 140-man unit, SS-Strumbannführer Kurt Gerickman nicknamed, "The Black Heart." He was an ordinary looking man of 40 who looked more like a tailor than a SS major. His vicious control and methods were well known to all in the area of Nancy. He was one of the original 300, the personal guard of Adolf Hitler formed in 1929 by Heinrich Himmler. The Reichsführer had seen his skills as an organizer in several operations including the phony radio station raid to incite furor against Poland in 1939. With Himmler's help, he quickly rose up the ladder of SS success.

Riding in the second staff car was his equally ruthless younger brother SS-Hauptsturmführer Otto Gerickman who was feared by all, especially the women of Nancy. No woman was safe, married or otherwise, if he wanted her for his pleasure. Local SS authorities always dismissed any protests or charges when brought by French citizens. Ten years younger than his brother, he was Hitler's perfect poster board Nazi cutting a dashing handsome character in his black SS uniform with his blue eyes and blond hair.

Kurt Gerickman's driver looked down at his temperature gauge. "Sir, we need to stop and let the car cool down. We are pushing the engine too hard."

"All right Heinrich, pull over there near that stand of trees," he said, pointing to a clear stretch of road a hundred yards on the right. The commander raised his hand signaling the rest of the column to pull over as well. They had been traveling since yesterday afternoon when it looked like the Wehrmacht would not be able to contain the Americans. As the vehicles came to a halt, the men piled out to stretch their legs while the drivers attended their vehicles.

The motorcycles had gone a 100 meters before one of the riders realized they no longer were leading the column. As they rode up to staff car, Gerickman ordered the SS man in charge of motorcycle unit, "There is a crossroads a few kilometers from here. Go ahead and check it out, then report back."

The cyclist gave a salute, "Heil Hitler" before heading back up the road.

Gerickman watched the two motorcycles leave for the crossroads while he lit a cigarette. Behind them in the distance, the rumble of artillery drew the attention of the unit. Gerickman's younger brother walked to the first command car. "They're getting closer. I don't think the Wehrmacht is holding them back, Kurt."

"You worry too much, little brother. We will escape the Americans. It is the duty of the Wehrmacht to fight and die for The Fatherland. It's the army's fault we are retreating. Our duty is to get to the safety of Strasbourg to continue the work of the Führer." There was fire in his eyes as he continued, "Remember our cowardly generals tried to kill the one man who can turn our current retreat into an enormous victory. Think of it. They tried to kill our beloved Führer with a bomb." He was referring to the July 20, 1944 attempted assassination of Hitler. "But the conspirators and their accomplices were discovered and eliminated. It is no wonder we are in retreat. The Führer ought to shoot every Wehrmacht officer above the rank of colonel and replace them with SS officers. Then we could win this war."

The younger Gerickman nodded his head in agreement. He didn't believe Goebbels' propaganda anymore but he knew better than to disagree with his brother about the untruths that were broadcast. He was a good Nazi but also a realist. He could read the signs, and the war was not going well.

"How far is it to Strasbourg?" Otto Gerickman asked with a hint of concern.

The older Gerickman opened his satchel case getting out his map to check their present location. He adjusted his wire rim spectacles. "According to this map, about eighty more kilometers," he replied.

Both officers were startled by the sounds of nearby gunfire coming from the bend in the road.

"My God, they are ahead of us!" Otto Gerickman blurted. "What do we do, Kurt?"

"Control yourself, Otto. It might be partisans. They're active in this area. Get the men to their vehicles."

After a few minutes, one of the motorcycles sped in their direction. Just as it reached the other vehicles it spun out of control spilling both the driver and his rider from the sidecar in the dirt.

They ran to the fallen cyclists. The passenger was obviously dead. Laying face up with three bright red patches across the chest of his black uniform, his lifeless eyes stared up at his commander. The driver was alive but had a badly shot up left shoulder.

"What happened?" Kurt Gerickman demanded.

"Americans at the crossroads . . . many vehicles . . . a company or more . . . Karl and Guenther killed . . . we barely escaped," he gasped before passing out.

"Pick him up and get him in one of the trucks," ordered Gerickman. Several SS men picked up the unconscious man carrying him to the nearest truck.

Pointing to the nearest group of SS men, "Who can ride a motorcycle?"

"I can, Herr Strumbannführer," Private Rauser replied.

"Good, check his cycle to see it still runs. If it does you take charge of it. If it doesn't start push it out of sight in the woods."

"Jahowl, Herr Strumbannführer,"

"What do we do with Private Klauser?" Sergeant Rolf Lohr asked.

"We don't have time to bury him. Hide his body in the woods."

"Otto, turn the vehicles around. We need to find a different route. We have to get off this road before the Americans spot us," Kurt Gerickman said.

"I saw a dirt road going southeast about two kilometers behind us," Otto replied.

The SS soldiers ran to their various vehicles to turn around to head west. The drivers gunned their engines making sweeping u-turns heading the opposite direction. Private Rauser righted the over-turned motorcycle and led the column towards the dirt road.

Gerickman thought to himself that he wished he had a battle trained Waffen SS unit instead of his own. They were garrison troops. No match for a battle hardened force, especially a motorized unit. They were used to bullying civilian populations not fighting combat units.

The SS column turned off on to the dirt road, continuing until all the vehicles could not be seen from the road. There was a small clearing where the dirt road left the main road, but the heavy growth of trees soon swallowed it. Kurt Gerickman ordered his men to stay in their vehicles in case a quick getaway was in order. He concealed himself in the brush close enough to watch the main road. There he waited until the sound of multiple engines was heard. It didn't take long for him to realize their situation as American light tanks and half-tracks sped down the road.

Through his binoculars, he watched two vehicles pull off the side of the road. Dismounting from the two jeeps several men pointed to the dirt road leading to Gerickman's unit. They seemed to study their maps trying to determine their location. One of the men handed a radiophone to his companion. After a few minutes, they got back in their jeeps and proceeded to follow the armored column.

The older Gerickman was soon aware that his brother and two other SS men had reached his hiding place.

"Did you see anything Kurt?" Otto asked.

"Armored vehicles heading fast to the west. We're cutoff. There is nowhere to go except to follow this road. Several vehicles stopped, but I don't think they're coming this way now," he hoped. "But I think they will send units this way eventually."

They hurried back to the group of vehicles, calling the officers together.

"This is the situation. We can't get through by way of the main road to Strasbourg. There is a group of Americans at the crossroads here," pointing to his map, "and at least a second column on the road to Nancy in the direction we came."

"This dirt road is heading for Colmar then turns north to Strasbourg, and we will follow it as far as we can. We will have to fight our way through if necessary," he said in as confident a voice as he could muster. The eyes of his men betrayed their fear of being caught behind enemy lines.

"Otto, I want one half-track to lead the column and the second to guard the rear. We will follow the first vehicle with our staff cars with the trucks in the middle. Any trouble we should be able to deploy quickly. Send Private Rauser on the remaining motorcycle to scout ahead."

He watched his men move quickly to their vehicles. He sensed that his men were not enthusiastic about their situation, but they would follow his orders. He wondered how they would react if they ran into Allied patrols. Few of his men had any combat experience. His men had four heavy machine guns plus two more mounted in the two half-tracks. His men were well armed with plenty of ammunition. If they ran into an enemy unit, would they fight or break and run?

His brother interrupted his thoughts. "We're ready to move out, Kurt. Do you want to ride together?"

"No, I want you to take charge of the other staff car," Kurt Gerickman said, lowering his voice.

"Do you think the men know what is hidden in the two staff cars?" Otto whispered.

"No, only you and I loaded the staff cars the night we left Nancy."

"In order to keep the men busy, I gave orders to round suspected trouble makers and to dispose of any of the prisoners we had incarcerated at Gestapo headquarters."

Neither of the two brothers noticed the three SS men who were watching their every move.

"They are keeping something from us," Corporal Heinz Mueller said with a puzzled look on his face.

"Maybe they are just concerned about being cutoff. I know I am," Private Guenther Schneider said.

"You know that Gestapo do not fare well if captured. Do you remember when Ernest disappeared on guard duty, and what we found the next day, his mutilated corpse. Just thinking about it makes me want to throw up," Private Walter Goehl said.

"Ernest was killed by partisans, but that's not it," replied Mueller.

They loaded into the last half-track. Mueller was not sure what was going on, but somewhere on the way to Strasbourg he was going to find out. He watched the two officers walking towards their staff cars no longer talking in whispered tones.

"Are there any towns between us and where the dirt road intersects the main road?" Otto Gerickman asked.

"Yes, there are several small villages." said Kurt Gerickman. "We should be able to reach the first village before dark."

"How far to the first one?"

"About fifteen kilometers down the road is a flyspeck of a village named . . ." Handing the map to Otto he asked, "Can you make out the name?"

"Nueviant," answered Otto.

After climbing aboard his staff car, Gerickman gave the signal to proceed to the village. The situation was not good but with some luck they might make it to Strasbourg. Unfortunately, they have had plenty of luck, all bad.

Chapter 3

Racing down the south road heading for the Strasbourg crossroads were elements of Patton's 6th Armored Division. In the lead was a jeep reconnaissance squadron of E Company, 6th Armored Battalion. With his Thompson submachine gun ready for use, Lieutenant Jack Wallace watched the French countryside looking for any sign of Germans. The twenty-six-year-old officer was in command of the lead unit of the northern pincer engaged in a mad race to cut off as many German troops as they could before they escaped to the east. The western pincer coming from Nancy contained elements of the 35th Division who were being held up by hard fighting German rearguard units.

Driving Wallace's jeep was Corporal Frank Pierson, a twenty-two-year-old steel worker from Pittsburgh. "How far to the crossroads, Lieutenant?" Pierson asked.

"Another thirty five miles. We should be there in twenty five minutes," Wallace replied, glancing at his watch.

They had been on the road for the last six hours trying to beat any retreating German units to the crossroads. The light resistance they had encountered was quickly eliminated and the race to the road junction continued.

In the back of the jeep sat Sergeant Jerry Rickett and Private Michael Goldstein with their weapons ready for action. "Looks like something big burning up ahead," commented Goldstein, at eighteen the youngest member of Wallace's outfit. As the jeep sped closer, they could make out the burning remains of a German column.

Rickett in his Texas drawl said, "Seems like the Air Corps beat the crap out of them."

"Just hope some trigger happy Luftwaffe pilot in a FW190 doesn't do the same to us," Pierson replied.

"You worry too much. I haven't seen nothing but our planes all day," Goldstein remarked.

"Kid, you better worry. You'll live longer," Sergeant Rickett urged.

"Sarge, I intend to live to a ripe old age." Goldstein chuckled.

Lieutenant Wallace softly spoke, "So did they."

Their smiles turned grim as they came close to the wreckage of the German column. The true reality of the airborne attack was now evident. Burning trucks, knocked out tanks and dead German soldiers in grotesque positions littered the road and surrounding fields. The vehicles were decorated with the logo of 25th Panzer Grenadiers. Corporal Pierson slowed down and began weaving back and forth through the carnage.

A young Wehrmacht officer lay sprawled out next to his staff car with that blank stare that always accompanies death. Wallace thought this kid looked young enough to have been on the high school football team that he coached in Detroit. They were soon clear of the wreckage, and they resumed the race to the crossroads.

Glancing at the gas gauge, Pierson suggested, "Lieutenant, we're riding on empty. We need to stop."

"OK, pull off into that apple orchard on the right."

Wallace turned to Private Goldstein, the radioman, "Inform Captain Neilson, we're stopping to gas up."

The other jeeps in the unit followed their lead and turned into the orchard. As the jeeps rolled to a halt, Wallace shouted to his men, "Take 10."

Goldstein and Pierson grabbed the spare gas cans and began filling the gas tank.

Wallace walked to a group of trees in the orchard. Tossing his helmet aside, he slumped down next to an old oak tree. Stroking his dark brown hair, he thought of his men and how to complete his mission without getting more of them killed. He took command of his platoon in July of 1944. At last count he had twenty-three of the original thirty-five men left. He got out his canteen and took a swig of warm water as Sergeant Rickett joined him under the tree.

The thirty-three-year-old Rickett was regular army having joined in 1930. He originally had been with the 1st Armored Division but had been reassigned as an experienced non-com when the 6th Armored Division was created. This tall and well-built Texan with his sandy hair and piercing blue eyes looked more like a matinee idol than 1st Platoon's top sergeant. Rickett was a highly decorated veteran with a Silver and two Bronze Stars, who was cool and calm in combat situations.

Wallace produced a pack of Luckies, offering a cigarette to Rickett. "What do think? Are there Germans left around here?"

Looking back to the smashed German column, Rickett replied, "I don't know. All depends on how much infantry were in the trucks on whether they would be an effective force. If only a handful survived, a few diehards might do some sniping at us but the rest will just try to get to their lines. But if the trucks were loaded with panzer grenadiers, they might setup roadblocks and ambushes."

Wallace had been a cocky 2nd lieutenant straight out of OCS when he first took command shortly after D-Day. After ignoring Rickett's advice and nearly getting himself and some of his men killed in their first combat action, he learned to trust his sergeant's instincts. The casualty totals would have been much higher if not for Rickett's experience. Many a time his advice gave his platoon that extra edge. Rickett as usual, his weapon always at the ready, watched the orchard for any sign of German stragglers.

Goldstein and Pierson were again arguing who was the greatest ballplayer of all time.

"Williams hit .406 in '41," Pierson exclaimed.

"What about Ruth or Gehrig? The Babe hit 60 homers in '27 and Gehrig hit 46 homers in '36 leading the Yanks to another World Series," Goldstein insisted.

Glancing at his watch, Wallace smiled at the constant banter of the two avid baseball fans. "Jerry, time to saddle them up," he said, standing and picking up his helmet and weapon.

Sergeant Rickett bellowed, "Mount up."

Just as they were climbing on board the jeeps, a shot rang out hitting the lead jeep in the right headlamp.

"Sniper!" Wallace yelled.

The men hit the ground, finding cover on the ground or behind the jeeps. They scanned the woods, hoping to catch some movement or the reflection of the sniper's rifle scope. In vain they looked for anything that might give his position before the sniper fired again. The sniper's second shot hit Corporal Pierson in the right shoulder as he moved to better cover behind a jeep.

"Medic!" Rickett called.

A soldier with a red cross on his sleeve and helmet ran up to the wounded man. Private Phil "Doc" Stazinski, the platoon's medic, removed Pierson's combat jacket and began to apply sulfur to the wound before bandaging it.

"How bad is it, Doc?" Wallace asked.

"Not bad, just a flesh wound. Another Purple Heart to impress the ladies," he replied with a grin.

Pierson winced in pain as he retorted, "I just wish they had less painful medals."

Turning back to the problem of the sniper, Wallace asked in a calm voice, "Did anybody see him?" A chorus of negative answers filled the air.

Sergeant Rusty Cooper, Corporal Will Higgins, and PFC Stan Glassman moved up to the first jeep.

"Rickett, take Baumann and go right. Cooper, take Glassman and swing around to the left." Checking his watch, the lieutenant continued, "I have 3:45. In three minutes, we'll hammer the woods for ten seconds then hold our fire. If our boy is still in there, he'll try to shift to a different location. You should be able to spot him."

As an after thought Wallace added, "Take him prisoner if you can, we could use the intelligence."

"Questions?" Wallace saw everyone understood the plan. "Ok, let's do it."

He watched his men disappear into the woods on either side of the suspected sniper's location. At 3:48 he raised his hand in the air to signal the covering fire. For the agreed ten seconds, rounds of ammo slapped the trees and brush in the sniper's general direction hoping to get a lucky hit.

"Cease fire." Wallace yelled.

He only had to wait a couple of minutes before the sounds of a few rifle shots and the crash of a grenade resounded in the woods. His men heard a familiar voice yell out, "Hold your fire. We're coming out." He breathed a sigh of relief when his four men emerged flanking a wounded German soldier holding his arm.

"Some more business for you, Doc."

"Right, Lieutenant," Stazinski answered, grabbing his medical kit.

"Goldstein, call Captain Neilson and ask what to do with our prisoner."

"Ok, Lieutenant."

Wallace then added, "Tell Baumann we need him to interpret."

Turning his attention to Sergeant Rickett, "What happened?"

"Right after you stopped firing, he made his move to a new location. We fired a couple of rounds, which forced him to take cover behind some fallen trees. After he was wounded by a grenade tossed by Cooper, he decided to throw in the towel."

There was genuine fear in the prisoner's eyes as they darted back and forth from Wallace to Rickett and back again. They watched Stazinski bandage up the prisoner's left arm as Corporal Baumann arrived.

"Ask him his name, rank and unit, Baumann."

"*Was ist Ihr name, rank und maßeinheit?*"

"*Obergefreiter Helmut Kramer des 25. Panzer Grenadiers,*" the German answered nervously.

"He's a lance corporal with the 25th Panzer Grenadiers."

"Which regiment and battalion?"

"*Welches regiment und batalion?*"

"*3. Bataillon, 119. Panzers.*"

"Ask him if that was his unit destroyed on the road."

"*Waren Sie Teil der zerstörten Spalte auf der Straße?*"

"Ja."

"Ask him how many left of his unit after the fighter-bombers attacked?"

"Wieviele überlebten der Luftangriff."

"Nur eine Handvoll meiner Kameraden entging dem Angrifff."

"Only a handful escaped the attack, Lieutenant."

"Ask him where did they go."

"Wohin gingen sie?"

"Sie nahmen unser verletztes und gehen für unsere Zeilen voran," the German answered, pointing to the east.

"They picked up their wounded and headed for their lines and left our friend here as a rearguard."

"Lieutenant, Captain Neilson wants to talk to you," Goldstein said, handing the radiophone to Wallace.

"Wallace here."

"Jack, proceed at once to the crossroads."

"What do we do with the prisoner?"

"What's his rank and unit?"

"He's a lance corporal of the 119th Panzer Grenadier Regiment."

"Did he give you any other information?" Captain Neilson asked.

"Only that a handful escaped with their wounded and are heading for their lines to the east," Wallace replied.

"Take him with you. We'll transfer him later to the rear."

"Right, Captain."

Wallace handed the radiophone back to Goldstein.

"Baumann, give the German some water then tie him in Cooper's jeep to make sure he doesn't cause any trouble."

"We're taking him with us?" Baumann asked with a puzzled look.

"Captain Neilson's orders. He is small potatoes not worth slowing down the advance."

"Ok, sir"

Baumann gave the German a drink of water and started him walking to the last jeep at the point of a rifle.

Once again Wallace gave the command to Sergeant Rickett to get the men loaded. Rickett seemed unsettled about something, which prompted the question from Wallace, "Something eating at you, Sergeant?"

"I don't like it, Lieutenant. This lone kraut takes a couple of pot shots at us, hitting a headlamp and slightly wounded Pierson. He could have easily killed one or two of us before we could react. And when we capture him, he freely gives the information when you ask him. He tells us only a couple of his friends got away, but the empty trucks in the column tell us close to company strength could have escaped. He says they went east, but I saw some tracks going northwest when we passed that kraut column."

"We'll have to stay alert," Wallace replied.

"Goldstein, contact Captain Neilson. Enemy in company strength. Possibly west of our vicinity. Proceeding to the crossroads."

Wallace climbed aboard his jeep hoping for once that Rickett was wrong and the German prisoner was telling the truth. It would be dark in a few hours, and they needed to secure the crossroads. He would have liked to send out patrols to locate that German infantry, but that would take time and time was not on their side. And how much equipment did they carry off? Do they have panzershecks or light mortars? He knew they could be running right into an ambush, but orders were orders. His thoughts were broken by the sound of the big Texan yelling, "Mount up."

"Goldstein, take over the wheel and keep it under 35," he ordered. Glancing over his shoulder, he asked Pierson, "How's the shoulder?"

"I'll live, Lieutenant." Then as an afterthought, "Maybe I could get a couple weeks leave out this?"

"Dream on, Pierson," Rickett said with a smirk.

The jeep convoy moved down the road at a slower pace, the men ready to deploy at the first sign of trouble. After about thirty minutes, they screeched to a halt at the crossroads. "Goldstein, contact Captain Neilson: we have reached the crossroads, no enemy activity," Wallace said.

Goldstein slipped out from behind the wheel, picked up his radio and called the company commander.

All that marked the crossroads was a fallen signpost with two pointed boards lying in a water-filled ditch. A couple of abandoned enemy trucks with broken axles had been pushed off the road. There were no signs of any Germans.

Goldstein replaced the radiophone. "Captain Neilson said to hold our position. He'll be here in fifteen minutes."

"Ok, we're home." Wallace said it loud enough for men in his immediate area. Then turning to Rickett, "Set up a defensive perimeter. Anchor each end with one of our .30 calibers."

"Right, Lieutenant," Rickett replied. The big Texan barked the orders as the men moved their jeeps into position forming a loose inverted half-moon facing the roads leading to Strasbourg and Nancy. Wallace didn't watch the placement of the tripod mounted machine guns knowing ahead of time that Rickett would set them up with excellent firing lanes. Wallace was looking at the road leading to Nancy that disappeared into the woods fifty yards from the crossroads. Was it his imagination, or was something coming up the road? Mixed in with the sounds of distant artillery and his own jeeps moving about, there was another sound and it was getting closer.

Wallace had about ten seconds to yell, "Take Cover!"

Two German motorcycles burst out the woods on the west road. A dozen men opened fire on the hapless black-clad motorcyclists whose passengers tried to return fire with their weapons. The lead cycle careened out of control as rider and passenger received the full brunt of the American response. The two men were flipped into the air like rag dolls when the cycle came to halt in a ditch. The second cycle managed to reverse course and headed back down the road towards Nancy.

Several of Wallace's men jumped into a jeep ready to pursue the remaining cyclist.

"Let them go. Our orders are to stay put and wait for the captain."

Sergeant Cooper checked out the fallen cyclists and reported back to Wallace. "Both krauts are dead, Lieutenant. They're part of an SS police unit." He handed Wallace their pay books and some official looking papers.

Wallace was slightly surprised after examining the papers. "Gestapo from Nancy, were they stragglers or the recon for a bigger unit?"

Cooper replied, "Hard to tell either way."

As they spoke, the sounds of approaching vehicles were heard behind them. Several light armored vehicles followed by E company's command jeep pulled up at the crossroads. Captain Paul Neilson jumped out of his command vehicle next to Wallace, motioning the column to keep moving. The short and stocky Neilson was a former train engineer from St. Louis, MO. He was a no-nonsense officer who was well-liked by his men. Neilson would always go to bat for the men in his company.

He glanced in the general direction of the wrecked cycle. "What's the story, Jack?"

"We surprised a couple SS motorcycles coming over the road from Nancy. Killed two on the first cycle, possibly wounded the others. The second cycle headed back down the road. We have some information for our boys in intelligence," replied Wallace, handing the papers to Neilson.

Neilson briefly glanced at them before tossing the material to a boy-faced lieutenant. "Get this to the S2."

"Any casualties?" Neilson asked.

"No, they didn't have much of a chance to return fire. "

"Is the 35th still hung up outside Nancy?" Wallace asked.

"Yeah, the krauts have heavily mined the road and have quite a few well emplaced 88s. They are in at least regimental strength plus a company of Tiger tanks. Any sign of that company of panzer grenadiers?"

"No, but Rickett's instincts tell him they're out there. What are our orders, Captain?"

Neilson produced a map from inside his combat jacket, opening it on the hood of his jeep.

"4th Platoon and your platoon will hold here until our Shermans reach you in the morning," he said, pointing to a location on the map. "I'm taking the rest of the company and heading for Nancy. Follow us after our heavy armor reaches you."

Getting into his jeep, Neilson said," I trust Rickett's judgment. Keep your eyes open and be ready for anything, Jack."

Neilson tapped his driver on the shoulder. "Let's go, Tommy."

The captain's driver cut in between a half-track and a tank destroyer as the pursuit continued. Wallace and Cooper watched the jeep disappear down the forest-encased road as they walked to the defense perimeter where Rickett joined them.

"The perimeter is set, Lieutenant. We have both roads covered," Rickett reported.

Wallace replied, "Good, it will be dark soon. Put every third man on guard duty, four-hour shifts. Unless the captain needs us, we stay here until morning."

"Right, Skipper."

A supply truck pulled off the road. The supply truck crew jumped out and began unloading gas cans. A tall and lanky corporal walked over to Wallace. "What do you need besides gas, Lieutenant?"

"We could use M1 ammo and some .30 caliber belts for the machine guns. Any grenades in here?" he said, looking into the back of the truck.

The corporal nodded and climbed inside the back of the truck. He soon returned with the ammo and grenades that Wallace requested.

"Anything else, Lieutenant?"

"How about food and cigarettes?"

"Out of cigarettes but plenty of C-rations and K-rations." After the corporal unloaded several cases of each, he tossed a box of chocolate candy bars to Wallace. "How about these?"

Wallace smiled broadly. "Now you're talking, Corporal."

Wallace took several bars out before tossing the box on the crates of ammo and food.

"Goldstein, you and Glassman pass out the ammo and food. Be sure everybody gets some of those candy bars." He remembered the last time Goldstein passed out candy bars, half of them mysteriously disappeared.

His meaning was not lost on the young soldier who replied, "OK, Lieutenant."

The supply truck crew climbed back into their rig and rejoined the convoy. The column of truck-laden infantry and light armored vehicles passed through the crossroads. Wallace knew the heavy armor was at least four hours behind this column.

He set his helmet and Thompson next to him as he slumped along his jeep. He began to drift off when he became aware of a hand on his shoulder. He looked up to see Rickett and Goldstein standing over him.

"Captain wants you, Lieutenant," Goldstein said, offering the radiophone to Wallace.

He was a little woozy as he stood up taking the phone. "Wallace here, Captain."

Rickett watched Wallace's facial expressions change from sleepy to concerned, as he listened to Captain Neilson. Something told Rickett that their short visit at the crossroads was over. Wallace handed the radiophone back to Goldstein.

"What's up, Lieutenant?" Rickett asked.

"Captain found a dirt road a couple of miles down the Nancy road heading south. Wants us to block it to make sure no krauts try to slip out that way. We'll leave Cooper in charge here while we take 1st squad to watch that road. In the morning we'll take a patrol south until we make contact with the krauts if any are out that way."

"One squad? Captain knows there are a lot of Germans moving around, doesn't he? We can get our cans kicked, but good," Goldstein insisted.

"Thanks for volunteering," Wallace said.

"But, Lieutenant I'm —," Goldstein started to complain, but a smiling Rickett cut him off.

"The Lieutenant needs a radio man, and you're it, Goldstein."

Goldstein grabbed the radio and began grumbling all the way to his jeep.

Rickett watched the kid kick the tire of his jeep as he told Wallace, "One of these days that kid will learn to keep his mouth shut. But he's right; one squad could really get caught in a bind out there."

"I know it, Jerry. That's why I want one of 4th Platoon's machine guns and its crew to come along with us. We will need the extra firepower if we run into those panzer grenadiers. Cooper will have the heavy armor support to back him up if the krauts attack the crossroads. Get the men ready. We leave in five minutes."

"Ok, Lieutenant."

Wallace shook his head, God help them if they found that missing Wehrmacht company. Goldstein could be right. Twelve men against possibly hundred combat veterans, this could be a suicide mission.

Chapter 4

The panzer grenadiers slowly moved out of their assigned positions as the black BMW staff car pulled up to the church. Strumbannführer Kurt Gerickman strode out of his vehicle with his crisp black uniform. On his chest an array of non-military Nazi decorations, at his waist his most prized possession, his SS dagger.

"Heil Hitler." Weselmann said. He disliked the SS, but the situation dictated proper protocol.

Gerickman's contempt was obvious as he returned the salute with the wave of his gloves.

"Heil Hitler, Sergeant. Who is in command here?"

"I am, Herr Strumbannführer."

"And who are you?"

"Unterfeldwebel Franz Weselmann, 25th Panzer Grenadiers, sir."

"What are you and your men doing in this village?"

"Our unit was cutoff when the Americans broke through our lines. We are trying to rejoin our regiment."

"Rejoin your regiment? Or are you and your men cowards running from a fight?" Gerickman said, unconvinced of their purpose.

"I assure you we are not running from a fight but will rejoin our unit in its new defense position, sir."

"I should hang you and your men for being deserters. We are losing this war because the Wehrmacht keeps retreating."

Weselmann felt his hand tightening on the stock of his MP40 but thought better of the idea.

"Very well, Sergeant. You no longer need to find your unit. I'm ordering you to defend this village should the Americans come this way. It will be dark shortly, so my unit will stay the night."

Gerickman's tone even though unpleasant gave Weselmann some relief. He thought at least he isn't going to hang us as deserters.

"Are there any other people in this village?"

"Except for a couple of nuns, living in the church, the town is deserted, sir."

"My men are going to use the church for the night. Move them out to one of the houses."

Weselmann bit his tongue. "I'll take care of it, sir"

"You may set your sentries out for the night. Do not try to leave. My men will be watching. Carry on, Sergeant."

Weselmann sharply saluted, "Yes, sir."

As Gerickman walked away, Weselmann was relieved. He was sure the Gestapo was going to solve the problem of how to get back to his regiment. Entering the church, he went to the basement where the two nuns were residing.

"Sister Monique?"

"Yes, Sergeant," a soft voice called from a dimly lit part of the basement.

Sister Monique stepped out of the darkness as Weselmann continued.

"A German unit has occupied the village and wants to use the church until tomorrow. You and Sister Genevieve need to move to one of the houses until they leave in the morning."

"Are you still angry with me, Sergeant?"

"No, I was concerned for your safety. I apologize for yelling at you."

Regardless of the situation, she put warmth in his heart and was glad to have the opportunity to be in her company again.

"I'm glad a German unit is here. You can now join with them and find your regiment."

Weselmann's facial expression changed from a smile to a frown.

"What is it, Sergeant?" Sister Monique asked.

"The unit is," he paused for a moment, "SS Gestapo."

The look on her face told Weselmann that she understood the seriousness of the situation.

They didn't seem to notice Sister Genevieve leaving the basement while they spoke. The first indication that she was no longer in the basement was the sounds of catcalls and commotion coming from upstairs.

Weselmann and Sister Monique ran up the stairs to find a half a dozen SS men laughing and pulling on the older nun. They turned and looked at Weselmann. And though they outnumbered him six to one, Weselmann's icy cold stare told them they best not continue their game. He escorted the two nuns past the SS men who went back to bringing supplies and equipment into the church.

Once outside they found the older Gerickman and his brother waiting for them.

"I am SS-Strumbannführer Kurt Gerickman, and this is my brother SS-Hauptsturmführer Otto Gerickman. We are going to need the use of this building for the night. Please get whatever you need for you will not be allowed to return until we leave. If you do not interfere with us, you will have nothing to fear."

"God will protect us. I know we have nothing to fear. We have what we need," Sister Monique replied.

"Very well. Carry on, Sergeant."

Weselmann did not like the look that the younger Gerickman was giving Sister Monique.

The trio walked to the last house, the one nearest the eastern end of the village. Weselmann's men had come together in front of the first house, milling about trying to figure out what was their next move. Looks of concern were on their faces.

After the nuns entered the house, Vopel spoke up, "What did the Gestapo scum want, Franz?" Vopel was no friend of the SS. He had family members who were arrested by the Gestapo and never seen again.

"Typical Gestapo intimidation, but they need us to cover their butts should the Americans come this way. For a while I thought, the way he talked, he was going to shoot us for deserting." Weselmann replied.

"Fighting for Germany is one thing, but fighting for the likes of these is what I can't stomach, Sergeant," said Stempel, spitting on the ground.

"None of us like the situation, but hopefully the Gestapo will leave before the Americans get here, Grandpa," Weselmann replied.

"Why don't we just leave?" Baake asked.

"I don't have to look over my shoulder, but I imagine there are several SS men watching us now. Their commander Herr Gerickman told me not to try to leave."

"Gerickman?" Vopel sighed, "Isn't his nickname The Black Heart."

"He's the one."

"Not good, Franz. Gestapo is bad enough, but he's one of the worst. One of Himmler's pet officers."

"Aren't the Gestapo on our side?" Piontek asked.

"Son, they're on nobody's side but their own. They would shoot you on the spot if it would save their butts without blinking an eye," Vopel replied.

"What are we going to do, Sergeant?" Rotter asked.

"For right now we are going to set up guard posts. Corporal Vopel, will you assign the men?"

"Yes, we mustn't let any partisans slip in to cut a SS throat or two can we, Sergeant?" Vopel said sarcastically.

"No Hans, that would make Herr Gerickman very upset."

"Bunzel and Baake, take the first watch. Piontek and I will relieve you in three hours. Rotter and Stempel, take the last watch," Vopel ordered. "Those not on watch can sleep in the house with the yellow awnings."

Weselmann went to the house occupied by the nuns and knocked on the door. Sister Monique called through the door, "Who is it?"

"Sergeant Weselmann. I just wanted to make sure you and Sister Genevieve were all right."

Sister Monique opened the door and stepped outside into the cool evening air.

"Sister Genevieve is asleep. Unless it's her garden, nothing seems to bother her. I talked about how the SS men treated her in the church, but all she was worried about was whether the night air was good for her tomato plants."

"And how are you feeling?" asked Weselmann.

"These men frighten me. Unlike your men who seem decent in many ways, I sense that these SS men are evil, especially their officers. I have heard of atrocities committed by the Gestapo, but to have them here in our village, in our church, and to talk to them is terrifying."

"I know our people fear and dislike the Gestapo as well. I've fought side by side with Waffen SS troops and found them fanatical soldiers. Some committed unspeakable acts in the heat of battle, but these men kill and murder on whims. Killing unarmed civilians is as routine as swatting flies to them."

Weselmann realized the conversation was upsetting the young novice and decided to change the subject. "Enough talk of this war. Are you from this part of France?"

Sister Monique was glad the young sergeant changed the subject. "I was born and raised near Colmar. My grandmother was German, from a town in Bavaria," she replied relaxing slightly, sitting down on a small bench in front of the house.

Weselmann perked up. "Bavaria? Where in Bavaria was your grandmother from?"

"I think it was Krumbac or something like that."

"Krumbach is only forty kilometers from my home town of Landsberg. What was her maiden name?" Weselmann asked.

"I'm sorry I don't remember that. Is it important?"

"No, I just thought I might have known some of your relations in Germany."

"You may sit down, Sergeant?" she said with that infectious smile.

Weselmann thought he should check the outposts, but her smile convinced him to stay a little longer. Hans knew his business.

The sentries would be placed in the right location. He unbuckled his cartridge belt and then set his helmet and MP40 on the bench as he sat down.

Glancing towards the south side of the village, he noticed that Gerickman had posted his own sentries guarding the church.

As dusk turned to night, the trees took on a ghostly glow as the full moon rose into the clear sky.

"It looks like it will be a beautiful night. This part of France isn't much different than Bavaria," he said, wishing he was back home right now.

"Autumn is beautiful, but winter has always been my favorite time of year."

"Why winter? Do you ski?"

"Yes, I was quite good. Jacques," she paused for a moment, "and I would spend most of the winter on the slopes."

"Was Jacques your husband?" asked Weselmann, seeing that tears were starting to form in her eyes.

Sister Monique merely nodded her head. The conversation stalled as neither Weselmann nor the young novice knew what to say next. The two sat in silence for what seemed forever before Corporal Vopel walked up to them.

"Franz, the outposts are set for the night. You better get some sleep."

The sergeant nodded to his friend as he got up from the bench. He slung his cartridge belt over his shoulder then picked up his helmet and weapon. He was glad that Vopel had broken the tension of the moment.

Sister Monique rose off the bench turning towards Weselmann. She smiled and with a tear rolling down her cheek said, "Good night."

As she entered the house, Weselmann softly said, "Good night."

He stared at the door for sometime when Vopel said, "Franz, you coming in or are you going to sleep standing up."

"I'm on my way, mother."

Weselmann started for the door of the house his squad had occupied, when the distant sounds of a firefight were heard coming from the west. Vopel stepped out of the house asking, "How close do think, Franz?"

"Twelve to fifteen kilometers. Double the sentry posts. We may have visitors before morning."

Vopel stepped into the house. In a couple of minutes, Piontek and Rotter stumbled out of the house to reinforce the outposts.

Weselmann saw commotion down by the church, thinking the Gestapo must have heard the sounds as well. The two half-tracks pulled up in front of the church, while several squads of SS formed up in defensive positions guarding the flanks.

A Gestapo man ran up to Weselmann. "Herr Strumbannführer wants to see you."

The SS man ran back to the church while the two panzer grenadiers followed at a much slower pace.

"I wonder what Herr Gerickman wants us to do?" Weselmann mused.

"Probably wants the seven of us to launch a massive counterattack while he slips away," Vopel chuckled.

The two Gerickman brothers were standing just outside the church, using a flashlight to read a map, when Weselmann and Vopel arrived.

"It's about time. What kept you?" Kurt Gerickman said.

It was apparent he was irritated with the Wehrmacht soldiers.

"Had to make sure the outposts were reinforced properly, sir," said Weselmann as Vopel tried hard not to smile.

"Next time be quicker. Do you think the Americans will reach the village tonight?"

"I don't think so. I know I wouldn't blunder into a village at night without knowing the enemy's strength. I have reinforced our outposts in the event the Americans do attack tonight."

"Move all your men to the west road, just in case you are wrong," Gerickman ordered.

"Anything else, sir."

"No, that's all, Sergeant."

"Yes, sir."

Watching the two panzer grenadiers move off into the darkness, Kurt Gerickman said to his brother, "I don't trust this sergeant. Tomorrow when we leave I want you and a squad to stay behind to make sure they stay at their posts."

"How long do you want me to stay? I don't fancy the idea of being in the village when the Americans arrive."

"I plan to leave by first light, stay for about four hours. We will wait for you in the next village."

Kurt Gerickman pointed to a location on his map, but the younger Gerickman was more interested in the house that the nuns occupied.

"I imagine I can find something to keep me entertained until then."

The younger Gerickman had a cruel looking smile on his face.

Chapter 5

Hauptmann Hans Dietz wondered if the deception would work. From the edge of the woods, through his binoculars, he watched Lance Corporal Kramer being interrogated by the American soldiers who had just captured him. Kramer was too good of a soldier to lose, but his loss would be acceptable if he could convince the Americans that his unit had been destroyed by the Allied fighter-bombers.

He thought back to his conversation with Kramer of allowing the Americans to capture him and give false information. He told Kramer harass them but don't kill any. His chances of survival would be greatly enhanced if the enemy didn't have dead friends lying at his feet. Since the war started, he had lost many close comrades on the Russian Front to snipers. Personally he hated all snipers but especially the ones that killed and then surrendered after running out of ammo. In Russia, Dietz made quick work of any captured snipers. A quick slash across the throat with his knife solved the problem of taking them prisoner. Maybe Americans felt the same, but they hadn't killed Kramer and didn't seem they would, as a medic was bandaging his shoulder.

Dietz watched with satisfaction as Kramer pointed to the east away from were his men were hiding. The officers in charge listened to a soldier who appeared to be an interpreter in that only he talked directly to Kramer. The American also pointed to the east. The soldier then led the lance corporal to the last jeep in the formation where he was tied up and loaded into the vehicle. Dietz waited until the jeeps were back on the road heading for the Strasbourg crossing before walking back to his company.

Hauptmann Hans Dietz, commander of 2nd Company, 119th Regiment of the 25th Panzer Grenadiers, was the typical Wehrmacht officer. Tall and well built, the thirty-eight-year-old officer was a fourteen year seasoned veteran of Hitler's army. Decorated with the Knight's Cross for gallantry under fire, his name was already a legend in the division. An excellent company commander, he was fair to his men but cruel and uncompassionate to the enemy. With his blond hair, blue eyes, and chiseled features, he would have been an excellent candidate for the SS. But there were rumors of a Jewish great grandparent that excluded him from joining the Waffen SS.

He had told the battalion commander it was foolish to risk the road in broad daylight, but the major, straight from a staff desk, thought he knew better. Major Schlepe said the unit had to reach the crossroads before the Americans. Dietz had told him to hide in the woods until dark but he wouldn't listen. He, along with many good men, lay dead in the wreckage of the column. Fortunately the fighter-bombers concentrated on destroying the armor in the column before strafing the trucks. The major's command car was destroyed in the same explosion that destroyed the lead Panzer IV tank. Dietz's men, mostly battled tested veterans, immediately jumped down from the trucks and took cover in a drainage ditch close to the road. After the fighter-bombers flew off, his men salvaged as many weapons and as much ammo as they could carry. He ordered them to move 400 meters into the woods heading north while he stayed back to see if the deception would work.

He had walked fifteen minutes when he reached the outposts of his company scattered among the trees on the edge of a small clearing in the woods. Only a plane flying directly over them could have spotted any of his men. His officers gathered around him to plan their next move.

"Did the Americans take the bait, Herr Hauptmann?" Lieutenant Klaus Krueger, his aide, asked.

"I think so, Klaus," Dietz replied.

"What is our strength?"

Each platoon leader gave the effective strength of his platoon.

"1st Platoon, three dead, six wounded, twenty available."

"2nd Platoon, two dead, five wounded, twenty-five available."

"3rd Platoon, five dead, six wounded, eighteen available."

"4th Platoon, one dead, two wounded, twenty-six available."

"What do we have in support weapons?"

"Two 80 mm mortars with forty rounds, one MG 42 with 350 rounds, two MG 34s with 500 rounds, two panzershecks with seven rounds, and seven anti-tank mines," answered the leader of the heavy weapons platoon.

"What is the condition of the wounded?"

"More than half need immediate medical attention if they are to survive. The rest have serious wounds but not life threatening," one of the company's medics answered.

After studying a sector map, Dietz said, "We can't make a stand on the two main roads that lead to Strasbourg. Enemy-fighter bombers would destroy any roadblock because they would be too exposed from the air. According to this map, fifteen kilometers to the south is a detour that heads to a few small villages.

This dirt road is not much more than a trail, but after the villages, the road winds then rejoins the main road to Strasbourg after about another sixty kilometers. We are going to take that road."

"Are we retreating, Herr Hauptmann?"

"No, Kurt. We find an area of the road hard to spot from the air then dig in on both sides of the road and throw up a roadblock. And we hold that road for any German units trying to get to Strasbourg."

"For how long do we hold the road?"

"For at least two or three days. The enemy planes and artillery will be minimal in their effectiveness. We'll place the anti-tank mines in the road to halt any armored vehicles."

"Would it not be wiser to escape ourselves, Herr Hauptmann?"

Dietz eyes narrowed as he angrily answered Sergeant Ritter, "I'm tired of being pushed around. We stand and fight on our terms this time. Have you forgotten the beating our regiment has taken in retreat? Good men died uselessly in that column because of a fool of a battalion commander who wouldn't take good advice. Lieutenant Mueller, whose platoon you are now leading, is dead on that road.

If I am to die, I want to take as many of the enemy with me as possible."

A shaken Sergeant Ritter replied, "Yes, Herr Hauptmann."

Turning to the medic, "Take the badly wounded back to the main road where the Americans will find them. They will have a better chance in an American field hospital than with us. Any wounded that can still fight can stay with the company."

The medic nodded as he left to gather some soldiers to move the badly wounded men back to the field near the road.

"Assemble the men, we move out in ten minutes."

The pace was slow moving the extra equipment, but they reached the edge of the woods just before nightfall. To get to the other side, they would have to cross seventy-five yards of open field. Through his binoculars, Dietz could see the break in the trees where the dirt road should be located.

"We'll wait until dark before crossing to the other side," said Dietz. "Klaus, post some men to sentry duty, and let the rest get some sleep. Wake me in four hours."

"Yes, Herr Hauptmann," Krueger replied.

Dietz slumped down under a huge pine tree taking a picture of his wife and two children out of his tunic pocket. Looking at his family, he hoped they were safe and sound at his father-in-law's farm. When the Allied bombers began striking German cities, he had them moved to the country. Hanover was not a safe place to live. The children, Helga age seven and Karl age nine, were probably enjoying their grandfather's animals while his pretty wife Hilda looked on.

If only this war would end, he would gladly trade his soldier's uniform for a farmer's pitchfork. He had enough of Hitler's war, the slow destruction of Germany. The attitude of his men, with the exception of a few fanatics, had changed as well in that they no longer believed Hitler's promises. But they would fight and die for Germany if not for Hitler.

He closed his eyes letting himself drift off into sleep when his aide shook his shoulder whispering, "Herr Hauptmann, wake up."

"What is it, Klaus?"

"Americans at the entrance to the dirt road."

Dietz shook the cobwebs from his head. "What's their strength?"

"Looks like three jeeps and twelve to fifteen men."

He reached the tree line in time to see the Americans unloading equipment out of their jeeps. Pointing to a small clearing fifty yards from where they crouched, Dietz whispered, "Get the platoon leaders together. We'll meet over there."

"Yes, Herr Hauptmann."

Dietz looked through his binoculars watching the Americans setting up camp for the night. "Well lads, you interrupted my sleep," he softly whispered. "In thirty minutes, we are going to interrupt yours." When he put down his binoculars, there was an amusing smile on his face, as he quietly moved to his platoon leaders to explain the plan.

"Questions?" Dietz asked his men.

None of the leaders needed more explanation. The plan was simple enough. First, drop several mortar rounds in among the American vehicles. Second, send the 1st Platoon to the right and 2nd Platoon to left. Third, fire short bursts from the three machine guns to cover the advance. Either the Americans would retreat or stand and be destroyed.

The German officer watched the placement of the machine guns, walking to each crew reminding them that the object was to fire short bursts to limit the amount of rounds expended. The idea, he told them, was to push the enemy away from the dirt road not necessarily wiping them out.

Night had fallen on the French countryside as Dietz slowly turned to the mortar crew and in a muffled voice said, "Now."

The heavy hammering of the machine guns and the whistle of the 80mm mortar shattered the night sky. The first two mortar rounds bracketed the American unit. The third round was a direct hit on the lead jeep as it jumped in the air. Its gas tank exploded lighting up the area. In the light of the burning vehicle, Dietz could see the Americans scurrying around trying to organize a defense. A parachute flare shot into the air revealed 2nd Company's platoons circling the American position. Realizing their predicament, the Americans piled into the two remaining jeeps before they sped down the road in the direction of the small village listed on the sector map.

"Cease fire." Dietz ordered, waving his hands to halt the firing of the support weapons.

"Herr Hauptmann, they're running like hares!" Krueger exclaimed.

"Under the circumstances they're doing the only smart thing. If the roles were reversed you and I would be running. Tell Lieutenant Schmidt and Sergeant Ritter to bring up their platoons. The heavy weapons and the wounded can wait until we secure the position then have them cross the road."

Accompanying Schmidt's platoon, Dietz crossed the main road to the former American position. By the light of the burning jeep he could see scattered equipment everywhere.

"The Americans were fortunate we only hit one of their vehicles. There were no signs of any casualties," Lieutenant Schmidt remarked.

"Wait a minute, there is something over here," Kruger said.

"What is it, Klaus?" Dietz asked.

"Appears to be a field radio or what's left of one."

"Good. They do not have the ability to warn their comrades of our presence."

Crouching down to get a better look, Dietz noticed something wet near the radio.

"Blood, it appears to lead to where the other jeeps were parked. They were not as fortunate as originally thought."

"What are your orders, Herr Hauptmann?" Kruger asked.

"In ten minutes we will move down the road until we can find an area best suited for the roadblock. Leave a squad here for the night in case more enemy patrols arrive."

"Yes, Herr Hauptmann."

For the time being he allowed his men to rummage through the discarded American equipment which included candy bars, K-rations, C-rations, fresh socks and other items of interest.

After all his platoons crossed the main road, Dietz ordered the men forward.

He saw Sergeant Ritter leading his platoon towards the new position. Rolf Ritter was a good soldier. That was why he inherited the platoon after its previous commander was killed in the air attack. He had served with Dietz from the beginning since the Polish campaign in 1939 when Dietz was a platoon commander and Ritter was a squad leader. Dietz walked along with Ritter, wondering what his sergeant thought about the roadblock.

"You don't think it is a good idea to set an ambush for the Americans?"

"You must have a good reason for setting a roadblock on this road."

"If we continue to fall back, the Americans will just keep following. Sooner or later, we have to make a stand. Without trucks to transport the men we have no hope of outrunning the enemy. They would destroy us on the road if we continue to push for Strasbourg."

"Then the situation is hopeless," replied Ritter.

"No, not if we stick to fighting in the woods. Without their air support and artillery, we can fight the Americans on even terms."

"But for how long? Even with the captured supplies we only have food for three days."

"Hauptmann Hauser's 3rd Company was the rearguard. I'm hoping they can join us before pulling back."

"Then this is a delaying action instead of a last stand," Ritter said.

"I want to return home to Germany after the war just like the rest of the men. If in a few days there is no sign of Hauser's men, we will fall back. In the meantime we can give the Americans a bloody nose if they attack our prepared position.

After walking about hundred yards down the road Dietz said, "This is a good spot to halt the company. Krueger, where are you?"

A voice in the dark answered, "Here, Herr Hauptmann."

"Inform the platoon leaders we are stopping for the night."

Turning back to Ritter, "Your platoon provides security tonight. I'm sorry that I spoke harshly towards you, Rolf. That idiot Major Schlepe got himself killed before I could vent my anger and took it out on you."

Ritter nodded then went to set up the outposts for the night.

Staring into the inky darkness that swallowed the dirt road where the Americans had just fled, Dietz whispered, "You been chasing us half-way across France. Tonight was your turn to run for a while."

But deep in his heart, Dietz knew the war was lost. Our air support is almost non-existent, our tanks outnumbered five to one, the quality of German fighting troops was rapidly declining, Allied bombers blast German cities around the clock and soon the Allies would be at the last natural barrier before reaching the heartland of Germany. And it would not hold them for long. But the minor victory, small though it was, helped restore the morale of the men.

Chapter 6

The two jeeps sped down the narrow dirt road, bumping off small trees in an effort to escape the German assault. Wallace did his best in the lead jeep to avoid as many obstacles as possible. Rickett, in the second jeep, tried to keep up the maddening pace of his lieutenant. The two cramped jeeps, loaded with the twelve men, had gone about four kilometers when Wallace saw a small clearing coming up fast on the left. Braking hard, he turned the jeep into the clearing. Rickett used all his driving skill to avoid crashing into his lieutenant's vehicle. As he overshot the clearing, he drove off into a small ditch. The steering wheel spun out of his hands as a loud cracking noise came from under the engine.

Men piled out to setup a defensive perimeter around Wallace's jeep.

"Well, that was a hell of a wakeup call," Goldstein exclaimed.

"Goldstein, get a hold of Captain Neilson!" Wallace yelled.

"But Lieutenant —"

"No excuses. Get the Captain!"

Rickett ran from his wrecked jeep to settle down his officer.

"Lieutenant, what the kid is trying to tell you is the radio was in your jeep," Rickett explained.

Wallace turned and looked at Rickett not believing what he had just heard. Then the reality of their situation sunk in. He had forgotten the jeep that took the direct mortar hit was his own.

In the confusion of the moment he had jumped into the driver's seat of Corporal Higgins's jeep. All that mattered was getting the remaining jeeps and themselves out of mortar range.

"I don't how many kilometers we went, but I don't think they'll follow us tonight," Wallace hoped.

"I think you're right, they'll wait until daylight before moving down the road," Rickett replied.

"Goldstein, Baumann."

The two soldiers rushed up and listened intently to the lieutenant's orders.

"Goldstein, move fifteen yards east up the road. Baumann, move fifteen yards west down the road. Both of you, if you see any movement, don't fire just get back here quick. OK, move."

"Yes, sir."

Wallace watched the two men disappear to their assigned positions before turning to Rickett for his assessment.

"How bad did we get hit?"

"The new kid Malery caught some shrapnel from a mortar round. Doc is working on him now, but it doesn't look good. I have to check on the rest," a somber Rickett replied.

Noticing blood on Rickett's jacket, he asked in a very concerned tone, "Are you hurt?"

"No, it belongs to Malery. Some of us helped get him into one of the jeeps before we left," he replied.

Wallace knew better. He saw his sergeant lift the kid all by himself and still fight back at the same time. If they lived to get back to their lines, Rickett was going to get another decoration.

"You called it right again, Jerry."

"Sir?"

"I make it at least two machine guns plus fifty to sixty men. Saw them in the light of that flare we shot up. We found your missing company of panzer grenadiers," Wallace sighed.

"In addition to the men you saw, I figure another platoon in reserve," Rickett replied.

"Which ever it is, it's too much for us to go through."

Wallace took out his flashlight and the sector map. The two men ducked behind the jeep as they looked at the map, hoping the light wouldn't give away their position.

"This dirt road goes through a couple of villages before rejoining the main road. We have to follow it and rejoin our unit," Wallace said.

"What about cutting through the woods?" Rickett asked.

"I don't think so. According to the map, we're surrounded by thick forests; the only passable way for sure is the road. With no idea how many krauts are lurking about in the woods, our best bet is to follow this road. Check the men and our equipment, and then report back in ten minutes. I'm going to see how the kid's doing."

Rickett nodded, then left for the group of men digging in for the night.

Wallace walked to the back of the clearing to find Stazinski working on Private Malery's chest wound.

Doc looked up to Wallace and slowly shook his head.

"How's it going, Malery?" Wallace asked, trying to be as cheerful as possible.

The young soldier looked up at his officer. "I don't think I'm going to make it, Lieutenant," he said faintly.

"Nonsense, we'll get you back to a hospital then on a ship back home. In a couple of weeks, you'll be sitting on your porch with your wife and kid."

"Will you write," Malery coughed as his voice trailed off to a whisper, "my wife?"

"You can talk to her yourself, Malery."

Malery lifted his hand with all the strength he could muster. Taking the young soldier's hand, Wallace hoped the kid could hang on.

"Please Lieutenant . . . promise," he whispered as a trickle of blood rolled out the corner of his mouth.

Wallace said softly, "I promise, Malery."

With his lieutenant's promise, he closed his eyes and his hand slipped from Wallace's grasp.

"Doc." Wallace called softly.

Stazinski checked for a pulse. "He's gone, Lieutenant."

Wallace lowered his head saying something unintelligible under his breath.

"Lieutenant."

"Let's have it, Sergeant," Wallace said, wiping a tear from his eye as he turned.

"One badly wounded, eleven able to fight. Canfield took a flesh wound in the arm from one of the kraut machine guns. He'll be OK."

"The kid's dead."

"What?"

"Malery's dead."

"That's too bad. I liked that kid. Never gave anybody a lick of trouble. Always wanted to talk about his wife and kid."

"Where was he from?"

"Tulsa. He once told me he wanted to be a preacher someday."

"Do you have his address?"

"No, but the company clerk keeps all that information. Something I can do, Lieutenant."

"No, I promised to write his wife, and I will."

Wallace stared in the direction of the village. Malery is dead, can't do anything about that, but I can get the rest of my boys home.

"How about equipment and weapons?" a suddenly tired Wallace asked.

"One jeep is a washout, broken front axle. We still have the .30 caliber with five hundred rounds and the box of grenades. We're low on food and water. Most of the rations were in your jeep."

"Sentries are posted for the night. Let's try and get some sleep. Tomorrow is going to be a busy day, Sergeant."

None of Wallace's men slept well that night. Many in their nightmares relived the action that took place earlier in the night. They had arrived about forty minutes before dark, securing the dirt road from an attack from the direction of Colmar. After setting the outposts for the night, the men either started to catch some sleep or had a late night snack. They were rudely awakened to the sound of mortar rounds going off in their camp about thirty minutes after dark. The lieutenant fired off a parachute flare to reveal the advancing enemy closing in on two sides. Instead of defending a narrow road, they were faced with defending a wide perimeter with the Germans having overwhelming force plus mortar and machine gun support.

Shrapnel from the mortar round that destroyed the lieutenant's jeep also hit Billy Malery in the chest. Sergeant Rickett ran over and picked up the wounded soldier carrying him over his shoulder while firing his Thompson on the advancing Germans. Setting Malery in a jeep, he next grabbed the machine gun, tossing it in the back of the jeep.

"We're pulling out!" Sergeant Rickett and Lieutenant Wallace were yelling.

The men piled into the remaining two jeeps, firing blindly in the direction of the Germans. Hanging on for dear life, they arranged themselves the best they could in the jeeps while the drivers did their best to get down the road away from the ambush. Only the quick action of Rickett and Wallace saved the squad from heavy losses. The road —

A hand was on Higgin's shoulder, "Wake up. It's almost dawn."

Higgins looked up trying to focus, "Don't you ever sleep, Sarge?"

"I slept a little."

"What do you want, Sarge?"

"I need a volunteer for a walk."

"A walk? We're a jeep squadron. We have a jeep."

"Let's go, Higgins."

"All right, I'm coming."

Higgins, after grabbing his helmet and rifle, began jogging after Rickett.

"Sarge, we're going the wrong way. There's nothing but krauts behind us."

Ignoring Higgins comments, Rickett reached the outpost where Private Perry was stationed.

"See anything?"

"Nope, Baumann said it was quiet earlier and I haven't seen anything but a couple of squirrels collecting nuts, Sarge."

"We're taking a walk to see what the krauts are up to. Don't get trigger happy, I don't know how long we'll be. Let's use electric for the challenge and eel for the password."

Rickett and Higgins stayed close to the road but a good ten feet inside the woods where there was good cover.

They had gone about two kilometers when they heard the sounds of chopping trees and sawing. Getting closer they observed over twenty Germans hauling cut trees on to the road. In the dimly lit area, Rickett could see the multiple machine gun and mortar emplacements. Alongside the road additional panzer grenadiers were digging rifle pits.

"I've seen enough. Let's get back and tell the lieutenant," Rickett whispered.

Wallace was standing by the only remaining jeep when Rickett and Higgins returned from their scouting expedition. He didn't look happy.

"Have you heard of the chain of command? Maybe, you were promoted to captain in the last two hours," Wallace fumed.

"I couldn't sleep anyway and we needed to know what the krauts were up to, Lieutenant," Rickett said.

"Just don't pull anything like that again." Wallace replied angrily, "Well, what did you find out?"

"They're not retreating this way. They're digging in. About three kilometers to the west is where we saw the krauts building a roadblock. Their commander knows his business, picked a good spot in the road. Plenty of tree cover, it will be impossible to spot from the air. Even if we had a radio, the air corps couldn't knock it out. Our only hope is to head east. One more thing, a column with tracked vehicles used this road in the last forty-eight hours."

Gathering the men together, Wallace started to explain their situation.

"According to the map, we're about ten kilometers from a village called Nueviant. We'll put as much of our equipment as we can in the jeep. We'll drive to within a kilometer of the village where we'll hide the jeep in the woods. From there we'll proceed on foot. We should be able to scout the village without the krauts knowing we're in the area."

"Unless the outfit that clobbered us last night radioed ahead," Rickett commented.

"For that matter, we were close enough last night that they might have heard the gunfire," Wallace replied.

Wallace folded his map and then stuffed it in his pocket. "We move out in five minutes. Goldstein, you drive the jeep. Canfield, you ride with him."

The men got their gear together and assembled on the dirt road.

"Baumann, take point."

"Goldstein, keep it in first gear, keep a normal walking pace."

"Right, Lieutenant."

Behind Baumann, came Rickett and Jenkins.

"Don't bunch up. We don't want to give the krauts an easy target."

Wallace's men spaced themselves out about five yards apart, a man on either side of the road.

"What do you think of our chances, Sarge?" asked Private Jenkins.

"It'll be rough, but we'll make it. The krauts behind us aren't going anywhere, and the villages ahead may be deserted," Rickett replied.

"Won't the captain come looking for us?"

"Well he'll figure it out, when we don't report in, that something happened to our radio. Next, he'll send either Cooper's outfit or somebody else up that road right into the roadblock, unless we can get to a radio to warn them. Captain Neilson knows his business. He'll probably smell out an ambush."

"What about us? Won't he try to get to us?"

"When the captain sees how many Germans have the road blocked, with no radio contact from us, he won't know where to look for us. Just concentrate on your job," Rickett replied, a grim look on his face.

Private Terry Jenkins stared straight ahead not wanting to continue the conversation. He was from Buloxi, Mississippi. A possible major league prospect, he was playing shortstop in the Midwest League when he was drafted. At six feet two inches one hundred and sixty-five pounds he was tall and wiry and could throw a grenade farther than anyone else in the platoon. At nineteen, he was the second youngest member of the platoon.

"Don't worry kid. We'll get home. I plan to see you play in the big leagues when the war's over."

There was a sign of relief on Jenkins' face.

"OK, Sarge."

The cool morning air was slowly changing into the humidity of the day as the backs of their uniforms became stained with sweat. The sky was clear except for the occasional cumulus cloud that blocked the sun giving the men a little relief from the heat.

When Wallace felt they were within a kilometer, he signaled Goldstein to pull off the road. There was an area just big enough to conceal the jeep. Tossing all the unnecessary equipment in the jeep, they cut enough branches to quickly conceal its location. Wallace gathered his men together near the hidden jeep.

"We're within a kilometer of the village. From here on, no unnecessary talking," Wallace said in a quiet voice. "The village may be deserted or crawling with krauts. It's a tossup. Move out."

Looking down, Wallace saw the telltale signs of the tracked vehicles. The ground was hard packed dirt and there was no way to be sure if the tracks were made by tanks, self-propelled guns, half-tracks or armored cars. The image of Panther tanks loomed in his mind. He prayed to God that he was wrong.

They proceeded until Baumann knelt down. Wallace signaled the men to disperse into the woods on the right side of the road. Along with Rickett, he moved up to join Baumann. The road turned to the northeast where they could see the beginnings of a clearing.

"Rejoin the squad," Wallace whispered.

Entering the woods, they crawled as close as possible to the clearing without exposing their position.

They both froze at the sound of heavy footsteps. Pressing themselves close to the ground, they waited until the sound was gone. Rickett raised his head enough to look at the village. He then tapped Wallace on the shoulder. Twenty yards to their left was an outpost manned by three panzer grenadiers who were watching the road. A black uniformed sentry was walking north past the German position. At the east end of the village, several vehicles were gathered around an old church with more black-clad soldiers milling about them. Two more sentries were posted to the south.

"How many did you count? I make it fifteen," Rickett whispered.

"Could be more in the houses." Wallace replied.

"I think we can take them, Lieutenant," said a confident Rickett. "First, we take out the three sentries then toss a couple grenades into the outpost. As soon as the grenades go off, Goldstein drives the jeep in with three of our guys firing Thompsons. The rest of us give covering fire from the woods. They won't know what hit them."

"What if the grenades miss or a sentry cries out alerting the rest? The guys in the jeep would be history," a troubled Wallace replied.

"Our boys are good, Lieutenant. The guys in the jeep will be fine."

"OK, it's 10:34. We'll hit them at 11:00. I'm going back. Keep an eye on them."

Wallace started backing away from the clearing when Rickett whispered, "Lieutenant, wait a minute. Something's up."

There was an order from an officer standing by the church as the black-clad sentries left their posts and jogged for the vehicles. The three panzer grenadiers seeing the sentries leave, picked up their weapons and walked up to what appeared to be a storefront with a weather beaten sign reading *Boulangerie De Damme*.

"Looks like they're pulling out. We won't have to fight for this village after all, Sergeant." a relieved Wallace whispered.

Lieutenant Jack Wallace couldn't have been more wrong if he tried.

Chapter 7

An hour before dawn Weselmann left the house to check the outpost at the western end of the village manned by Vopel and Bunzel. SS sentries had been posted by Gerickman to make sure Weselmann and his men didn't try to disappear into the woods. As he approached the outpost, the strong aroma of a pipe was in the air.

"Smoking that stinking pipe again, Hans?" Weselmann said.

"Of course, my one vice in life, Franz," Vopel answered.

The coolness of the morning air gave life to their breaths. Weselmann slipped into the outpost, which was no more than a few logs hastily thrown together. The ever-vigilant Bunzel lay huddled close to the logs, rubbing his arms trying to keep warm. Had they really expected an attack during the night, a more elaborate defense would have been set.

"Doesn't it bother you that it gives away your position?" Weselmann asked.

"The three of us are behind a few logs out in the open, almost on the road itself. The Americans would have to be blind not to know we're here, Franz."

The black of night was slowly lifting as the sun began its ascent in the east. Weselmann could see the outline of the dirt road in the forest. Instead of a solid dark mass of black, the woods began to produce individual trees and bushes.

"If the Americans were close, they would've hit us by now. Be ready to fall back if they do show up, you'll have a better chance in the woods than in this exposed position. I want live grenadiers not dead heroes."

"Sounds more like Rommel everyday, doesn't he? Yes sir, I will do my best not to get killed." Vopel chuckled.

"What are our chances, Sergeant?" Bunzel asked, his eyes betraying his fear.

"If the SS lets us attend to our own affairs, we'll be all right," Weselmann replied, trying to assure the troubled youth.

"With me at your side, how can anything go wrong?" a smiling Vopel said, slapping the young grenadier on his shoulder. Bunzel cracked a small smile, relieved at least for the moment.

"I'm going to check on the rest of our men. If Herr Gerickman asks where they are, tell him I sent them back to get something to eat," Weselmann said, "He expected all of us to be at the outpost all night.

"Right, Franz."

Weselmann was glad he had Vopel in his unit. The man was a good soldier but his greatest asset was his humor in tight situations, which always kept the unit's morale up. Bunzel had asked their chances. With the Americans close behind them and the Gestapo in front of them, they were not good, but he was keeping that to himself.

As he walked to where his men slept, Weselmann remembered fishing with his grandpa on mornings like this. He thought of getting to the riverbank before dawn, the thrill of catching fish and listening to his grandpa telling his fish stories. He then wondered if he would have grandchildren to share a morning such as this one or if he would even live past this week.

The SS men were busy as well in the pre-dawn light, loading their equipment into the various vehicles. Two of them exited the church with the golden candlesticks from the church altar. Weselmann could only imagine the other religious and personal items that were being looted from the church.

An over-weight, out of breath SS non-com hurried to Weselmann wheezing, "Strumbannführer Gerickman wants you now, Sergeant."

Weselmann followed the SS man to the steps of the church, where the Gerickman brothers were arguing about something.

They immediately stopped their confrontation when they realized Weselmann was close enough to hear them. Just inside the church doors, the Wehrmacht sergeant noticed the SS men disassembling a radio receiver.

"I'm leaving in a few minutes with the majority of my men. We were in radio contact with a Wehrmacht unit blocking the dirt road about fifteen kilometers to the west. The firing we heard was a fight with an American patrol. They are somewhere in these woods. Hauptsturmführer Gerickman is staying behind to make sure you don't desert your post. Obey all his orders. Then when he leaves, you can take your men and try to rejoin your unit. Do you understand, Sergeant?" Kurt Gerickman said.

"Yes, sir. May I inquire which unit is blocking the road?"

"I believe it was a Hauptmann Dietz, do you know him?"

"Yes, sir. Hauptmann Dietz commands 2nd Company of our regiment," Weselmann replied, a hint of excitement in his voice.

"Carry on, Sergeant."

Weselmann saluted and went about his business. Something inside told him not to trust the Strumbannführer, but he couldn't do much about it. At least 2nd Company was in the area.

Kurt Gerickman waited until Weselmann was well out of hearing range before speaking again. "Otto, before you leave this village, I want you to hang that sergeant and all his men. Hang them, in the trees close to this church, as a warning to the Wehrmacht to think twice before retreating."

"What if they resist?"

"They won't because I want you to give them the impression of false security. Just before arresting them, give the sergeant permission to join their comrades at the roadblock. The fools will be off guard and you should be able to capture them without a fight when they assemble together," said a grinning Kurt Gerickman.

"Why not arrest them now?" Otto asked.

"There are Americans somewhere in the woods. We might still need Sergeant Weselmann and his men. There will be plenty of time later for your assignment, brother. "One more thing, be sure you hang his men first. I want the sergeant to see his men die before him. Then as an after thought, he said, "Oh, I have decided to take both staff cars with me."

"I think not, Kurt. I will not be cheated out of my fair share. Perhaps you would like the Americans to capture the village before I leave."

"Nonsense, Otto. Think of it as protecting your assets and I do outrank you. The staff cars go with me."

The conversation between the two officers began to draw the attention of their men, which was not lost on Kurt Gerickman.

"Perhaps the men would like to know what we are carrying." Otto smirked.

"Lower your voice, Otto. Very well, keep the staff car with you," a worried Kurt Gerickman replied. He knew if the men found out what they carried, they would have to share or have their throats cut by their own men. Even then some of his men might want it all.

"Is there anything else, Strumbannführer," his younger brother grinned.

"Just pick a squad of men to stay with you," Kurt Gerickman said.

"The equipment is loaded in the trucks. We're ready to go whenever you want to leave, sir," a young Gestapo lieutenant reported.

"Thank you, Kliest."

Gerickman headed to his staff car, watching Weselmann call his men together. Weselmann would have hope for about four hours. He wished he could see the look on his face when the sergeant's world came crashing down all round him. With that on his mind, he climbed aboard his staff car giving the signal to move out to his aide, who was sitting in the front seat next to the driver. The aide motioned the motorcycle rider and the driver of the nearest half-track to take the lead.

"Let's go, Heinrich," he ordered the driver. The big BMW staff car moved into position behind the half-track and quickly sped out of the village. Truck after truck followed in the column until only the second half-track remained, then it too disappeared down the road.

The seven panzer grenadiers met down by the outpost. Weselmann waited with his news until all the men were present.

"Will you tell us before you burst, Franz," a wondering Vopel said. The smile on Weselmann's face was hard to suppress.

"The firing we heard last night was Hauptmann Dietz's 2nd Company. They're dug in about fifteen kilometers west of here on the road."

"Glory be! What are we waiting for? Why don't we get down the road and join them?" Bunzel asked.

"We still have orders to guard the village until the rest of the Gestapo leave," Weselmann replied.

"Why if 2nd Company is blocking the road, do we have to hold the village? We can do more good with the rest of our lads at the roadblock," Vopel wondered.

"Hauptmann Dietz attacked an American reconnaissance patrol last night. The Gestapo wants us for protection, in case the Americans come near the village. Once the Gestapo leaves, we can linkup with the lads in 2nd Company," Weselmann explained.

"Until we pull out, I want Piontek, Rotter and Stempel in the outpost. Corporal Vopel and Private Bunzel get to our quarters and get a couple of hours of sleep. Baake come with me. We're going to the church."

Weselmann still didn't like the idea of the Gestapo still being in the village, but at least the senior Gerickman was gone. The man gave chills to Weselmann even when he sounded friendly. Not that the younger Gerickman was much better, but he didn't unsettle Weselmann like his brother did.

As they approached the church, a couple of rough-looking SS men stopped them at the entrance.

"No one enters the church, Herr Gerickman's orders." Weselmann recognized him as the same overweight non-com who spoke to him earlier.

"I need to post a man in the belfry, Sergeant," an annoyed Weselmann stated.

"I have my orders, no one is to enter the church," the non-com stated, training the barrel of his MP40 at Weselmann's midsection.

"Come, Baake we'll find another spot for you," Weselmann said, seeing the situation could get out of hand very quickly.

They walked back to the bakery, where they met Corporal Vopel and Bunzel. The two men had grim looks on their faces.

"I told you two to get some sleep," an irritated sergeant said. "I expect you to follow orders, especially you Corporal Vopel. You're useless to me if you're half asleep."

"We both tried but with the Gestapo crawling around, who can sleep? Look they have posted sentries around the village," said Vopel. "Are we protecting them or are they guarding us?"

"I know something's amiss. I don't like it but I can't put my finger on it. Something doesn't add up. I know that before Gerickman contacted Hauptmann Dietz, he was concerned about the Americans reaching the village. But with 2nd Company guarding the road, nothing is going to get through for a few days. He could easily have taken his entire force and headed east. And Herr Strumbannführer was almost friendly this morning. I think he's setting us up for something. Spread the word, expect anything at any moment from either side," Weselmann replied uneasily.

"Franz," Vopel said, tapping Weselmann's shoulder.

Weselmann turned and looked in the direction his friend was pointing. The two nuns were talking to the SS men, trying to enter the church. The heavyset SS man was shaking his head and pointing with his weapon towards the house where they spent the night. Weselmann hurried to them before the SS man did something he would regret. He would see to it.

"Sister Monique, please come here," he shouted.

The two nuns turned and walked towards him. The SS men seemed relieved that Weselmann was intervening.

"Sergeant Weselmann, these men will not let us enter the church. Please order them to let us in," Sister Monique pleaded.

"I'm sorry I can't countermand the orders their officer gave them. In a few hours, they will be gone, and then you can enter the church," he said in as soothing a voice he could muster. "Please stay in the house until the Gestapo leave. If you give them cause in their minds, they might do you harm."

"Very well, we will wait until they leave." said Sister Monique, taking Sister Genevieve's arm. Weselmann watched the two nuns enter their temporary quarters. He then walked towards the squad's house. In a few short hours they could move out to join 2nd Company.

Reaching the house, he tossed his helmet on the ground and unbuckled his belt. Rather than enter and wake anyone sleeping, he sat down on a stool and leaned against the wall, keeping his Schmeisser on his lap. It didn't take long for him to drift off.

Weselmann woke with a start. The three men from the outpost were standing in front of him. Still half asleep he groggily said, "What's the problem, Herr Hauptmann?"

"Wake up, Franz." Vopel said, shaking Weselmann's shoulder.

Weselmann shook his head trying to get the cobwebs out. "Hans, what's going on?"

"Gerickman's pulled in his sentries. I think they're ready to pull out."

The Gestapo had two vehicles, a kubelwagen and a truck parked near the church. Six Gestapo men were at the back of the truck, with their rifles ready for action. In the kubelwagen, behind the wheel, was another SS man. Absent were Otto Gerickman and the two men who had been guarding the church.

"Assemble the men, but be ready for trouble," Weselmann cautioned.

The words were hardly out of his mouth when suddenly there was a high pitched woman's scream that came from the house where the nuns were quartered. The two missing SS men were standing near the front door of the house. Gerickman's staff car was parked along side on the road.

"The nuns!" Weselmann shouted, sprinting for the house.

Otto Gerickman exited the front door, buttoning the front of his black tunic. A look of satisfaction was etched on his freshly scratched face. The three men, unaware of Weselmann's approach, had found something amusing as they stood in front of the house.

Uncontrollable anger swelled up in Weselmann as thoughts raced through his mind of Sister Monique and what this SS officer had done to her. He was losing all rational control and he didn't care.

Otto Gerickman, starting to head for his staff car, saw the rage and anger in Weselmann's eyes. He had time to say, "This is none of —," before Weselmann's fist slammed into the Nazi's gut, knocking him to a knee.

The SS officer regained his balance in time to receive a crushing blow to his face that slammed him backwards into the door forcing it open. Inside were the two nuns, one was lifeless on the floor and the other was trying to cover her semi nude body with the remains of her habit.

Gerickman rose to his feet, blood pouring from a broken nose.

"How dare you strike a German officer!" Gerickman shouted, fumbling to draw his Luger from its holster.

Gerickman stared in horror as the nimble Weselmann quickly brought up his MP40, firing a burst that caught the Hauptsturmführer in the throat. He sank to his knees trying to stem the flow of blood with his hands, looking at Weselmann with incredulous eyes. He pitched forward as death overtook him.

The overweight non-com tried to swing his machine pistol to avenge his commander but Vopel was quicker. A short burst to the chest and the big SS man slumped against the wall of a small shed, leaving a trail of blood as he fell.

The remaining SS man out of loyalty to his officer or stupidity, no one would ever know, tried to unsling his rifle from his shoulder. Disregarding a shout from Weselmann to stop, he continued until the sharp crack of Baake's rifle ended his action and his life.

The men at the truck immediately ran to the house at the sounds of gunfire. When they saw their downed companions, they opened fire standing in a row like a firing squad. Weselmann's men whirled, taking cover wherever available and quickly disposed of the Gestapo men.

Weselmann shouted, "The kubelwagen!"

The driver, after seeing his comrades slaughtered, decided there was no point staying any longer. Despite the shower of lead, he was able to escape the panzer grenadiers. The fight had lasted less than a few minutes but had cost the lives of nine men.

"That tears it. What'll we do, Franz?" Vopel said, finally at a loss of a humorous comeback.

"Collect the weapons and ammo. Search those vehicles for anything we can use." Weselmann ordered.

Weselmann hurried to the nun's house. Inside Sister Monique, clothed in a torn habit, was placing a sheet over the other nun. Kicking aside the feet and boots of the late Otto Gerickman, he closed the door. "How did this happen?" He asked in as soft a voice as he could.

She looked at him, with tears in her eyes, sobbing, "He came to ask if there was anything he could do for us. He was very polite and proper at first. He asked again was there anything he could do and placed a hand on my shoulder. I pulled away and asked him to leave. He just grinned and moved closer to me. That's when Sister Genevieve tried to stop him. He shoved her aside. She tried again and he pushed her hard into the fireplace," Weselmann looked to the fireplace seeing a dark red stain on one of the corners as she continued, "He pulled . . . he pulled at my . . ." Unable to continue she broke down crying on his shoulder.

He waited several minutes holding the troubled woman, hoping he could console her. "I'll send a couple of my men to bury the good sister. Please stay here until my men check out the village. There may still be some Gestapo in the church," he said, sitting her down on a chair by the table.

He left the house, looking down at the crumpled figure of Gerickman. Stepping over the body, he spat, "Welcome to Hell, Herr Hauptsturmführer."

Weselmann called all men together. "I'm sorry I got you all in this. It would have been better if I had given up after killing Gerickman."

"I don't think so, Franz. "There was something we found when checking the truck," Vopel replied.

"What did you find?"

"Seven ropes suitable for hanging, each with its own noose. They were planning to hang the lot of us. If anything, your actions saved us from a necktie party," said Vopel, showing one of the ropes.

"Necktie party?" Rotter asked.

"It's American slang for a hanging. I have family in America who write and tell us about their customs," Vopel replied.

"Find out anything else?" Weselmann asked.

"Yes, their wireless was in the truck. But it was hit by some random shots. It's useless," Baake replied.

"Well when they get the news about this firefight, they won't be able to radio to Hauptmann Dietz to arrest us, but Gerickman may send part of his men to either arrest us or try to contact our unit at the roadblock. I doubt if Dietz would hand us over, but there's always that chance," Weselmann speculated.

"How's our ammo?"

"We're in better shape now. We have twice as much than when we started this morning," said Vopel, handing Weselmann three full clips for his MP40.

"Where's Grandpa?" Weselmann asked, looking around.

"I don't know. I sent him to check out the staff car," Vopel replied.

"All right, let's spread out and look for him," Weselmann ordered.

"There he is, Sergeant," Bunzel yelled.

At the house where the fight started, Private Stempel was wildly signaling the men. Content they were on their way, he went back to staring in the trunk of the car.

The rest of them jogged up to the staff car. Vopel was the first to arrive. "What was so import—" His question was cutoff by his own whistle. As each man reached the car, his comments or actions were similar.

In the trunk were three small cases, one for franc notes, one for golden rings and earrings and one for assorted jewels.

"How do you think he accumulated so much treasure?" Baake wondered.

"Nancy probably acted as a collection point of the Jewish population from Southern France before being deported east. Any Jews that came through Nancy were stripped of their belongings. Any prisoners taken during that period were stripped as well. I imagine Herr Gerickman and his brother have been robbing civilians since 1940. No one ever speaks of it, but we all know what's happening to the Jews," Vopel said.

"What are we going to do with this loot, Franz?" Vopel asked.

Piontek jumped in, "Can't we keep it?"

Bunzel asked as well, "It belongs to us now, doesn't it?"

Looking at the two youngsters, Weselmann said in a firm tone, "If we keep this for ourselves, we are no better than the Gestapo. I would like to think the seven of us are better than the Gerickman crowd."

"What do we do with it, Franz?" Vopel asked again. Weselmann scanned the village until his eyes rested on the church.

"We hide the cases in the church basement. The first order of business is to make sure Herr Gerickman doesn't get it," Weselmann said.

"Are you sure Gerickman will come back, Sergeant?" Baake asked.

"Even if he won't come back for revenge, I think he will for the treasure. If I read him right, the man's greedy. He'll come back for the treasure."

Weselmann's face reflected sorrow as he remembered his promise. "Gerickman killed Sister Genevieve. I need a couple volunteers to bury her?" Weselmann asked in a somber tone.

After a slight delay, Baake and Bunzel raised their hands.

"Where do you want us to bury her, Sergeant?"

"Bury her in the garden near the spring," pausing for a moment Weselmann's face brightened. "I think she would like that."

Bunzel and Baake entered the house while Stempel, Rotter, and Piontek picked up the cases and headed for the church. Weselmann wondered if he convinced his men to give up the ill-gotten goods. He hoped so. They were a good bunch of lads.

"Where in the church, do you want to hide these cases?" Grandpa asked.

"There are basement stairs to the right at the front of the church. Take the cases and hide them in the second storage room. When you're done with that, carry the dead Gestapo into the woods," Weselmann ordered.

Vopel and Weselmann discussed the best way to defend the village. Each scenario ended in too few men and weapons to defeat Gerickman's unit.

They entered the church to take a better look from the steeple; they were appalled at the condition of the church. Anything of value had been taken. The statues of the saints were all broken as if it was some kind of amusement for the SS during the night. Behind the altar, the broken tabernacle lay with the wafer hosts scattered on the floor. If there was a chalice, it was missing. The pews had been wrenched from their permanent positions and had been shoved together into makeshift beds. Only the cross with the image of Jesus, that overlooked the sanctuary, had not been damaged.

"What kind of animal does this to a church?" Vopel sneered. "We're fighting for the likes of these, the Führer's new order."

Weselmann righted the broken tabernacle the best he could. He then found an empty cup and knelt down picking up the hosts, after which he placed them back in the tabernacle.

Piontek ran into the church, skidding to a halt after tripping on some broken furniture. Grabbing the edge of a pew to keep from falling to the floor, he blurted, "Sergeant Weselmann, the Americans are here! Hurry, they're here with a white flag."

An incredulous Weselmann and Vopel looked at each other, then they both ran out of the church.

Chapter 8

With Rickett at his side, Wallace watched the firefight through his binoculars, trying to figure out what was going on. The black-clad soldiers were quickly killed by what seemed to be a squad of panzer grenadiers. After the fight the green-clad soldiers hid the bodies of the dead men in the woods, and then they assembled by the old church.

"What do you make of this, Jerry?"

"I don't know, Lieutenant. Could be one of our O.S.S. units working behind the lines or a group of partisans using kraut uniforms."

Scanning the village with their binoculars, Wallace and Rickett both came to the same conclusion that only seven soldiers remained, milling around the church. Quickly they returned to their men hidden in a small clearing in the woods. The men gathered around Wallace as he began to brief them on the new situation.

"What was all the shooting, Lieutenant?" An inquisitive Goldstein asked, cradling his M1 in his arms.

"A change in plans," Wallace said, ignoring the kid for the moment. "The firefight in the village was between two groups of krauts. Might be some of our guys in German uniforms. I need a volunteer, who speaks some German, to enter the village under a flag of truce with me. Any takers?"

The incredulous look in their eyes told Wallace that his men thought he had lost his mind. The more he thought about it maybe he had. It was only a ten percent chance that the men in the village weren't Germans, but he wanted to be sure. There was a long pause before anyone spoke.

"I'll go," Rickett said reluctantly.

"No, if anything goes wrong, I want you in charge here," replied Wallace. "Anybody else?"

"Count me in, Lieutenant."

"All right, Lepper."

Twenty-four-year-old Corporal Tom Lepper was a former electrician from Toledo, Ohio. The tall and lanky soldier could always be counted on when the chips were down.

"Sure you want to do this, Lieutenant?" Rickett asked. "More than likely, they're krauts. I've seen them use a white flag to ambush our boys in Africa. They'll let you and Lepper walk close to them and then open up."

Wallace took a knife from his belt, cutting a young sapling. As he sat down, he began stripping the branches off before attaching a white handkerchief to it. "How many men have we lost to friendly fire?" he said, looking at his sergeant.

"Two weeks ago Stevens and Baker were killed coming back from night patrol. Our sentries thought they were Germans, opening on them before they could give the password. They didn't have a chance," Rickett replied, remembering a bad situation.

Satisfied the truce flag was sufficient, Wallace stood up. "That's right they didn't have a chance," he said, handing his Thompson to Rickett. "I had to write their parents that they died in action. I couldn't tell them that some of our own jittery sentries shot and killed their sons. I plan to give these men a chance, besides I'd like to know why they were fighting the SS."

Rickett's eyes glanced to the ground as he reflected on Wallace's words. "Ok, we'll cover you from the woods. But any sign of trouble, hit the deck and we'll open up on them."

"Sounds like a plan. Let's go, Lepper."

The sun felt warm and comfortable on his neck as he walked up the road towards the village. As he and Lepper reached the bend in the road, the first couple of houses became visible. Another ten paces and the whole village came into view. He felt like he was in an old western waiting for the outlaws who hid in every corner of the town to jump out for a fight.

"Keep that white flag up high where they can see it," he reminded Corporal Lepper.

Wallace was brought back to reality when a few Germans, who were stationed near the church, noticed him and Lepper walking past the abandoned outpost. A flurry of guttural shouts told the lieutenant they were German soldiers. At that moment the wisdom of his decision came into question in his own mind. Too late to turn back, he decided to go through with the original plan. The two Americans headed for the old church.

Two German soldiers walked briskly towards them. Wallace could tell by their appearance they were combat veterans. Both men wore wound badges and the Iron Cross for bravery on their dirty tunics. The taller of the two soldiers snapped to attention. "Unterfeldwebel Franz Weselmann," he said in perfect English. "What can I do for you, Lieutenant?"

Wallace returned the salute, saying in his most commanding voice, "Surrender. My men have the village surrounded and we outnumber you five to one. You can save the lives of your men by not fighting against hopeless odds." Wallace was hoping a bluff could help the Germans into surrendering.

"Lieutenant, I know that you are only in squad strength. We had news of your encounter last night with Hauptmann Dietz's company," a slightly amused Weselmann replied. "You are in as much trouble as we are, cut off behind our lines between two superior forces."

"Unterf—," Wallace stumbled in pronouncing the Wehrmacht version of Weselmann's rank.

"That's a sergeant in your army, Lieutenant," Vopel interrupted seeing the American wasn't comfortable with the German rank. Vopel's English wasn't as good as his friend's but was clearly understandable; Wallace nodded his thanks before continuing.

"I don't think you and six men would be considered a superior force, Sergeant." Wallace said with a grim face. "My men still outnumber your unit."

Weselmann looked to Vopel saying in German, "Hans, should I tell him?"

"I would just like to see the look on his face," Vopel chuckled back in German.

"Mind telling me what the joke is, Sergeant?" An irritated Wallace asked.

"No doubt, you saw the fight with the Gestapo. Well there are a hundred or more headed this way in about two hours, looking for blood. The driver in the kubelwagen escaped to tell SS Strumbannführer Gerickman, excuse me Major Gerickman, what happened to his brother."

"You killed his brother. Why?"

Weselmann glanced in the direction of the house where Sister Monique was probably still sobbing. Looking back to Wallace he softly said, "I had a reason."

"Reason?"

Weselmann opened his mouth but the words wouldn't come. Vopel put his hand on his friend's shoulder, taking over the conversation the best he could.

"There were only two villagers left when we arrived yesterday, a couple of nuns. They were very kind to us, especially Sister Monique. Then the Gestapo," Vopel spat on the ground, "showed up, taking over the town. Most of them left this morning heading east, but a small unit stayed behind under Gerickman's brother. We heard a scream. Sister Genevieve had been killed and the SS captain had molested Sister Monique before Franz could stop him. After Franz knocked him to the ground, Herr Gerickman drew his pistol. Well, you know the rest, Lieutenant."

"In about two hours we'll probably be dead, I can't imagine a way to hold our position with only seven men. Herr Gerickman has over a hundred men plus two armored half-tracks," Weselmann added.

"Why don't you just leave the village?" Wallace asked.

"Gerickman knows my name, as well as Corporal Vopel's name. If we run, he will avenge himself on our families. I have given permission for my men to leave, but they refuse to go. I suggest you and your men disappear into the woods and pretend we never had this conversation, Lieutenant."

"How do we know you won't radio your friends to look for us?" Wallace asked.

"Piontek."

"Yes, Sergeant."

"Bring the radio to the lieutenant."

After the young soldier retrieved the radio, Wallace realized that it had been damaged beyond repair. With the lack of a radio, there was no way for Weselmann to warn anyone.

"Does that satisfy your concern?"

Wallace nodded his head in agreement. "We could take your men prisoner and try to get to our lines. That way we could save your life and those of your men."

"No, that would be the same as running away. Gerickman would track our families down," said Weselmann, thinking he could be out of this war.

Both men realized there was nothing else to do. The two Germans came to attention as Weselmann said, "I think that concludes our business, Lieutenant."

"Good luck Sergeant. Hope you and your men can somehow get out of this mess."

As Wallace and Lepper turned to walk away, Vopel made a remark that froze Wallace in his tracks. "Too bad you're not on our side, Lieutenant. We might have a chance to beat off Gerickman with an extra squad of men."

"What did you say, Corporal?" Wallace asked, an idea popping into his head.

"Only that if we were on the same side, we could defeat the Gestapo," Vopel replied with a puzzled look on his face.

"What kind of commander is your Hauptmann Dietz?" Wallace asked.

"He's a typical German officer. I don't know what you mean," Weselmann replied, looking to Vopel who hunched his shoulders.

"I mean will he fall back or hold his position?"

"Dietz will hold until he has to retreat or runs out of ammunition, but what's this got to do with anything?" Weselmann asked.

"Ok, my problem is getting my men home to our company. We are cutoff between two superior forces without adequate transport. Your problem is you are about to be overrun and killed. How about using the corporal's suggestion and team up temporarily to save the lives of our men."

"A truce," Weselmann responded, his eyes lighting up. "But why would you help us? We are your enemies," Weselmann pressed, hoping the American lieutenant had the right answer.

"Because the best chance my men have to live is to go through the SS up that road. It is also the best chance you and your men have to survive. Separately our units could be wiped out, but together as a unit we can limit our casualties to a minimum. We destroy the Gestapo unit and my men take one of their trucks and rejoin our unit. You are then free to rejoin your unit. Hopefully we will never see each other after this truce expires," Wallace replied.

In the distance, from the direction of the roadblock came the sound of an artillery barrage. The two men's attention turned towards the west.

"What if another American unit arrives before we destroy Herr Gerickman's unit?" Weselmann questioned.

"If that happens all bets are off. You and your men head for the woods as fast as possible. The same would go for me and my men if a German unit showed up unexpectedly."

"What do you think, Hans?" Weselmann asked his friend.

"Have you two gone mad? We were trying to kill each other yesterday. How can we put our men together?" Vopel asked in a skeptical tone.

"It's really simple. We have a common enemy, the Gestapo," said Wallace, trying to sell Vopel. "Who would you rather kill, us or the Gestapo, Corporal?"

"Lieutenant, personally I have nothing against Americans. I would like to move there someday but right now we are at war with you."

"Corporal Vopel, assemble the men. Tell them to hold their fire, the Americans are coming in." Weselmann ordered.

Wallace watched the Germans line up in parade formation in front of the church, with slung weapons. Vopel wasn't happy about the decision, but he was obeying his sergeant. Weselmann began to brief them on the decision.

"Lepper, tell Sergeant Rickett to bring in the men and our equipment. Be sure to tell him to hold his fire. The situation is under control," said Wallace, thinking Rickett is not going to believe this.

"You going to be all right, Lieutenant?"

"Yeah, I'm fine. Be sure Sergeant Rickett tells our guys not to fire. Hurry Lepper, we only have an hour and a half to get ready."

Wallace lit up a cigarette as he sat down on the church steps. Feeling all the German eyes on him, he flipped his pack of Luckies to Weselmann. After a nod from Wallace, he distributed them among his men. Weselmann then sat down next to the American lieutenant.

"Thank you, Lieutenant," said Weselmann, handing the half-empty pack of cigarettes back to Wallace. "If we might die together, I think it would be good to know your name."

Wallace realized he had never given Weselmann his name.

"Jack Wallace."

As Lepper disappeared into the woods, Wallace could visualize the encounter with Rickett. A similar display of total unbelief on the part of his first sergeant, but like Weselmann's corporal, he would obey orders.

The first indication that Rickett was on the move was the sound of Goldstein's jeep coming around the bend, followed by the rest of Wallace's men. The jeep skidded to a halt at the church, as Rickett sprinted up to the two men sitting on the steps.

"Begging your pardon, sir. But have you lost your mind? These are enemy soldiers, how can we expect them to fight against their own men?"

"Take a look inside this church. My men would never do such destruction to God's house. No, only the Gestapo would do such a thing. They are not like my men, Sergeant," Weselmann replied.

Rickett walked up to the open doors of the church to see the destruction wreaked by the Gestapo. He shook his head with disgust at what Gerickman's men had done to the place. Most civilized men show respect for a church or synagogue, but the Gestapo represented the worst in men.

"Sergeant Rickett, this is Sergeant Weselmann and Corporal Vopel," said Wallace, doing the introductions.

Rickett nodded to his German counterparts. "But why are we considering fighting the Gestapo with them, Lieutenant?"

Finishing their cigarettes, Wallace and Weselmann stood up.

"Assemble your men and brief them on what we are going to do, Sergeant."

"Sergeant Rickett, gather the men together, I want to explain the situation to them."

The men moved into two groups facing each other, in front of the church. A line of panzer grenadiers in dirty green uniforms on the right and a line of Americans in their equally dirty olive drab uniforms. Their eyes remained glued on their respective opposite numbers. Weapons were ready if anyone made a false move. They listened as Wallace and Weselmann explained the situation to their own men. The more they explained the plan; the more the tension seemed to ease. Even Vopel and Rickett seemed to see the plus side of the truce.

Individual soldiers slung their weapons as a sign they would obey Wallace and Weselmann. Soon only Goldstein and Bunzel stood facing each other, weapons at the ready.

"Goldstein, you got a problem?" Rickett shouted as he moved towards the infantryman.

"Sarge, I'm Jewish and I've heard the rumors of what they are doing to all the Jews they can find," said Goldstein without taking his eyes off Bunzel. "I can't fight for them."

Vopel moved to Bunzel's side, whispering something to him that caused the young panzer grenadier to lower his weapon and walk to the church.

Turning to Goldstein, he said, "The rumors are true. The Gestapo has done terrible things to the Jews in Europe and Russia. But, I swear to you that none of the Wehrmacht soldiers before you have done any harm to your people. I had a favorite uncle who preached the unjust treatment of the Jews in Germany in 1938 from his pulpit. The Gestapo arrested him and my family still does not know his fate. Gerickman and his friends have killed and murdered hundreds if not thousands of innocent Jewish and non-Jewish civilians."

Goldstein lowered his weapon and walked to a small group of his friends without saying another word to either Vopel or Rickett. Wallace watched the kid, heaving a sigh of relief that Vopel had defused a nasty situation.

"I appreciate your help, Corporal. You just saved our temporary truce before it started," Wallace said.

"I didn't say anything that wasn't true. We fight for Germany, not Hitler and his gang. Today I will fight with you, tomorrow who knows," Vopel responded.

"Cheer up, think of the stories you can tell your grandchildren, Hans," Weselmann smiled.

"You know I am a confirmed bachelor. What grandchildren do you mean, Franz?" Vopel joked as a grin returned to his face.

Rickett and Wallace walked to the two Germans, with a rough drawing of the village. To all concerned, it was odd to see Americans and Germans milling about trying to make the best of the situation. Vopel was the first to comment, "They look like young kids at their first dance trying to figure out how to talk to the opposite sex."

Even Rickett thought the comment was funny as he said, "So you kra—, I mean Germans have a sense of humor."

"Of course, two enemies fighting side by side against the Gestapo, now that's hilarious, don't you think, Sergeant Rickett," Vopel mused.

"I just think it's nutty, that's all," replied Rickett with a frown.

"Let's get a positive attitude about this, Sergeant. If you can't get along with Weselmann and Vopel, our men won't follow suit. I'm not asking you to like them, just work with them to get us out of this jam," Wallace said, slightly annoyed.

"Don't worry after we eliminate the Gestapo, we can start shooting at each other again, Sergeant," Vopel quipped.

The three men looked at each other before slightly smiling at Vopel's humor. Wallace thought to himself these Germans are not much different than our men, even likable. How many Vopels and Weselmanns had he killed or maimed since he took command? And if this doesn't work, after talking and joking with them, could he ruthlessly gun them down if the situation demanded it? At this moment looking into their eyes, he hoped it would work. To get as many of his men as he could back to the American lines, it had to work.

Chapter 9

Kurt Gerickman sat at a table in the village's only restaurant, playing with an empty wine glass. But there was no one to wait on the Strumbannführer. Unlike the previous village, it was deserted. The town, whose name escaped Gerickman, was just a series of dilapidated buildings whose occupants had taken anything of value with them. His men were bored as they waited for the vehicles under Otto Gerickman's command.

He should never have left Otto. He could have left Kleist or another of his officers to take care of Unterfeldwebel Weselmann. If Otto were here, they could continue to Strasbourg. *What was I thinking? As soon as Otto balked at me taking his staff car, I should have left Kleist to take care of Weselmann.* He could not even contact Hauptmann Dietz at the roadblock, because some fool left the only radio in the truck in Nueviant. Gerickman continued fondling the empty glass until he violently flung it against the restaurant wall. He leaped from his seat, knocking over the table. After venting his anger at the inanimate objects, he checked his watch.

The sound of a vehicle speeding down the road brought relief then concern as the single kubelwagen roared into sight. Gerickman and his men surrounded the vehicle.

"Where is the rest of the column and my brother?" Kurt Gerickman demanded.

The SS man was stricken with fear as he stood before his commander. "Hauptsturmführer Gerickman is dead. They are all dead," he stammered.

"The Americans," Gerickman sighed, noticing bullet holes in the scout car, as he turned away from the driver.

"No, Herr Strumbannführer, it was the Sergeant Weselmann and his men."

"What!" Gerickman screamed, spinning around.

All the color drained from the SS man's face. He opened his mouth to speak but the words wouldn't come.

"What happened?" Gerickman screamed again.

Picking his next words carefully the SS man said, "Your brother gave orders to get ready to leave. I got the kubelwagen out on the road, warming the engine. He then went to the nun's quarters to see if there was anything he could do for them. Then without any provocation, Sergeant Weselmann, with the aid of his men, killed your brother, Sergeant Heinrich, and Private Leermann. The cowards then turned their weapons on the men rushing to help your brother. Seeing that all my comrades were dead, I saw no reason to stay, so I came back to warn you, sir."

Gerickman's eyes narrowed as he took the Luger from his holster. Sticking the barrel under the man's chin he asked in a chilling voice, "How is it that only you survived?"

The man's eyes bulged as the Luger pressed tightly against his throat. He closed his eyes, waiting for the crack of the automatic.

"Sir, there was nothing I could do. The killings took less than a minute. Had I not come here to tell what happened, I too would be lying dead in the road. They tried to kill me as well but I was lucky. Look, sir, at the bullet holes," the man gasped, realizing he was pleading for his life.

The holes in the scout car convinced the SS commander that the man was probably telling the truth, at least about escaping with his life.

"Kleist!" Gerickman yelled, replacing the Luger in his holster.

"Yes, sir."

"Take this man and two squads. Go back to Nueviant. Kill Weselmann. Shoot him, hang him, beat him to death, or whatever you want, but I want his head. I want him and his cowardly men dead. Do you understand, Kleist?" With each word Gerickman became more enraged.

"Yes, Herr Strumbannführer. Heil Hitler!" The young lieutenant said, giving a sharp salute.

Then remembering his brother, Gerickman said in a calmer voice, "Bring the Hauptsturmführer's body back in his staff car, Kleist. Be sure you bring back both his body and his staff car."

"Yes, sir."

There was a flurry of shouts as a squad of men climbed aboard a truck. Kleist had a quizzical look on his face. He wondered what was so important about the staff car. The driver had his head resting on the steering wheel, worn out by his ordeal with Gerickman, when the lieutenant tapped him on the shoulder. "Let's go." The driver was glad to leave the village or more to the point he just wanted to be away from his commander. The kubelwagen bolted ahead of the truck, and it then sped down the road.

After the lieutenant left with his makeshift unit, Gerickman walked off towards the south woods. He was taking the loss of his brother harder than he thought he would. He reflected on the many times he had gotten his younger brother out of trouble. "Visiting the nun's quarters, what were you thinking Otto?" He knew someday that a woman would cost his brother his life.

Sitting in the cab of the half-track, with the inscription *Hilda* stenciled on the hood, Corporal Mueller watched Gerickman's every move. Only a deaf man in the next town could not have heard the exchange between their commander and the luckless driver.

"Herr Gerickman seemed overly concerned about his brother's staff car," said Mueller.

"He's probably upset about his brother's death, Ernest?" Schneider commented, cleaning the firing mechanism of the MG42 in the half-track's front gun mount.

"Yes, I can understand that, but why does he want his brother's staff car? We have plenty of transport," Mueller pondered sitting sideways in the driver's seat with his legs dangling out the open door.

"Maybe there were family heirlooms in the Hauptsturmführer's car," said Private Goehl, adjusting the carburetor.

"No, I think there is more to the Strumbannführer's concern than family photos and artifacts. Who helped load the officer's staff cars?" Corporal Mueller asked, continuing to watch Gerickman.

"I don't know. I was too busy rounding up last minute troublemakers on Gerickman's list," Goehl replied, slamming the hood down.

"The staff cars were already loaded. After we finished our business in the courtyard, we were ordered to load the trucks," replied Schneider, jumping down from the side of the half-track. "I remember thinking about loading the officers' cars but was told that they had taken care of it themselves."

"That's a good one, when was the last time the officers did any manual labor for themselves?" Mueller smirked, lighting a cigarette. "There's something they wanted no one else to know."

"I think you're right, Klaus. But what could they be hiding?" Schneider asked a hint of suspicion in his voice.

Mueller stepped out the cab of the half-track. "What was the first official act we did after we entered Nancy?" asked Mueller.

"We set up security for our headquarters and living quarters," replied Schneider.

"After that?"

"We secured a list from the mayor's office of all persons living in the area," Schneider said with a puzzled look.

"And who were we interested in the most?"

"People we thought would make trouble and the Jews. What's that got to do with what's in his staff car?" Schneider queried, seemingly more confused with each question.

"When we rounded up the Jews in the region for deportation what was the first thing they did?"

"They registered for deportation to the eastern camps."

"And?"

"They were transported to the railhead," Goehl said.

"And?"

"Sent east, I don't know where you are going with all this, Klaus," Schneider said.

Looking at his companions, Mueller smiled as he shook his head. Drawing his friends closer together he said, "The Jews, before boarding the trains, were told to leave their money and valuables at the tables set up at the railhead."

"But all that was sent to Berlin," Schneider said.

"Where was it kept before being sent?"

"In Herr Gerickman's office. But shipments were sent to Berlin every Friday on the train," Goehl remarked.

"But what if two enterprising officers set back a little of each shipment?" Mueller asked, already knowing a possible answer to his question.

"What about the records? The clerks wrote in a ledger every item they collected."

"Records can be changed," Mueller replied.

"Herr Gerickman wouldn't do that; he is a loyal Nazi. He would not betray the Führer," Goehl responded, still not believing the corporal's theory.

"I'm like Goehl, I don't think Herr Gerickman has been stealing from the Führer, but how can we prove otherwise?" Schneider asked.

"Who's on sentry duty tonight?"

"Ludwig, Hessmann, Goehl, and me. Why?" asked Schneider.

"I think it's time we took a look inside the trunk of that car," a determined Mueller replied.

Chapter 10

The first American attack on Hauptmann Dietz's position had failed. Evidence to that fact, were two knocked out light armored-vehicles and several dead men in olive drab laying in front of his prepared defenses.

Dietz had selected an excellent portion of the road to defend. The dirt road curved to a 90-degree angle. Any attacking force would have to make a right turn before being able to see any sign of his position. The trees formed a protective canopy over his men to keep Allied aircraft from spotting or attacking his men's fortifications. Even artillery would have a limited effect on his defenses.

Four hours before daylight his men had started chopping down and hauling trees, setting up a log tank trap and burying the anti-tank mines where they hoped the enemy tanks would venture. There wasn't a lot of room for armored vehicles to maneuver, so to break through his defense, the Allied tanks would be forced into the minefield.

But his first victory was not without cost as he watched his men carry dead panzer grenadiers to the rear. Several were familiar faces from past campaigns. They were the first to die, but he knew the Americans would be back in greater force with a more efficient battle plan. His dead comrades would soon have company. His youthful aide interrupted his thoughts.

"Herr Hauptmann."

"Casualties, Klaus?"

"Six dead, four wounded."

"Ammunition?"

"We used about ten percent of our ammunition and two panzersheck rounds, sir."

"How is the morale of the men?"

"They are confident we can throw back the Americans again." Lieutenant Klaus Krueger reported proudly.

"Advise the commanders to expect another attack within two hours. This time I expect a heavy artillery barrage before their assault. After informing their subordinates, have Lieutenant Schmidt and Sergeant Ritter report to me," Dietz said.

He was not as confident as his aide, but with the terrain in favor of his forces, holding out another day was still in the cards. As long as he could deal with the enemy heavy tanks, there was hope of delaying the Americans. Hauser's 3rd Company could still be trying to get through the enemy lines, and if Dietz could hold the road open, they might accomplish their goal.

As the two men approached, the drone of a recon plane was heard. Through a small break in the tree cover, Dietz saw the plane trying to spot his roadblock. Back and forth, the plane skimmed in low, trying to get a glimpse of the German unit.

Dietz hoped his previous order of not firing on any reconnaissance planes would be obeyed. As the plane made pass after pass over the suspected area, not a single shot was fired. Finally the plane, evidently unable to spot any movement or sign of the position, gave up and headed for home.

Turning to the two platoon commanders, Dietz rearranged his defense for the next round. Bending down he drew the unit's position in the dirt with a stick, outlining how he wanted the two platoons deployed.

"The Americans will probably try to flank our position from either the south or the north. We can expect an artillery barrage before they launch their next assault. Ritter, take your platoon and dig in here on our southern flank, with two of the machine guns to support your men, Dietz said etching the sergeant's platoon in the dirt. "I expect the attack to come from that direction."

"What brings you to that conclusion, Herr Hauptmann?" Schmidt asked.

"A logical guess, shorter trek for their infantry to move through the woods if they attack our southern flank. But just in case they don't do the obvious. Johan, I want your platoon here," Dietz instructed, pointing to an area just behind the northern flank. "You can move quickly either to protect this flank or act as our reserve to plug any breaks in the line."

Dietz stood up and looked at his watch. "You'll probably have twenty to thirty minutes before the artillery barrage. Get your men moving as soon as possible."

"Jahowl, Herr Hauptmann." They both replied, trotting off to their respective platoons.

Dietz toured his defenses, making sure the men had dug deep enough to protect themselves from the expected shelling. After ordering a few panzer grenadiers to dig deeper holes, he was satisfied the artillery barrage would have a minimal effect.

His earlier anger towards the late battalion commander had subsided, being replaced by the cool and competent leadership which he had shown his entire career. He no longer wanted to fight to the death as he had the night before, taking as many of the enemy as he could. Instead he only wanted to delay the Americans as long as possible, giving Hauser's 3rd Company a chance to escape to the east. He decided to hold until tomorrow morning. If Hauser or his men did not show up by then, he would pull back.

At the whistle of the first shell, he dove into his dugout yelling, "Take cover!"

Shells burst in the treetops, showering the area with broken limbs. A few shells slipped through gaps in the trees, violently shaking the ground. The sound of artillery was deafening, intermingled with an occasional scream of anguish as a shell or a falling limb found a human target.

Dietz pressed his face into the ground, covering the back of his neck with his hands. Small branches and shattered pieces of the tree limbs pelted his back and legs as he lay in his dugout. Just when he thought he would go mad from the shelling, it mercifully stopped.

He raised his head to see the company's medics helping several wounded men to the rear.

"Klaus!" Dietz yelled, spitting dirt from his mouth.

"Yes, Herr Hauptmann."

He was glad to hear his young aide's voice. He had hoped Klaus wasn't one of the dead or wounded from the barrage.

The sounds of small arms fire on his right, told him the Americans weren't wasting any time trying to pierce his defenses. The distinctive sounds of the MG34 machine guns answered the enemy advance. Evidently the Americans didn't catch Ritter's men unaware.

"Send a runner to Sergeant Ritter to find out his situation."

The majority of Dietz's men were already in their battle positions waiting for the enemy to appear from the lingering smoke of the barrage. His men had weathered the onslaught fairly well as only one or two shells had found its mark. One dugout did receive a direct hit. The only evidence of a previous occupant was a blackened helmet smoking in the shell's crater. The main fortifications remained intact. The barrage had been random as the artillery, without accurate information from either the ground or the air reconnaissance, could only target a general area and not individual targets. Many shells had fallen harmlessly a hundred yards from any German position.

"Herr Hauptmann," said a gasping runner.

"What's Ritter's situation?"

"Sergeant Ritter was attacked by at least a platoon of infantry, but the flanking attack has been beaten back, sir. The enemy took some casualties before pulling back."

"Our losses?"

"Four killed, sir"

Dietz thought this battle of attrition can only end in an Allied victory as his force continued to be whittled down. At this rate, a few more attacks and he would be forced to withdraw.

"Tell the platoon leaders to meet, in ten minutes, over there," Dietz said, pointing to an oak tree near his dugout.

The drone of a reconnaissance plane was heard again as Dietz's men hunkered down in their dugouts. The artillery had damaged the tree cover but if the men didn't move around, maybe the plane wouldn't spot them. If they had an accurate location for artillery and the fighter-bombers, the German force would be decimated.

The last communiqué that Hauptmann Hauser sent was that the American tanks had shattered his rearguard and he was retreating in the best order he could. That was two days ago and he had not sent any more messages. If he didn't reach Dietz's position in the next day, then he and his men would be assumed lost. Hauser was a good commander and his loss would be missed, but Dietz decided that he would hold until tonight then pull back under the cover of night. His first responsibility was to the men in his company.

When all the platoon leaders had arrived, Dietz began to explain his plan and how he wanted it carried out after nightfall.

"We can expect several attacks today. It is also possible that we will have another artillery barrage or air strike prior to that attack. We hold, and if necessary, counterattack to give the Americans the impression that we are holding to the last man. As you know we have held this road hoping Hauptmann Hauser's company will join us. Unless we receive any news of 3rd Company, we will retreat tonight as soon as it is dark enough to shield our intentions. Schmidt, your platoon will be our rearguard. Give us a two-hour head start before slipping away."

"Yes, sir," Lieutenant Schmidt replied.

"Schmidt, if attacked, fall back slowly. Delay them but don't stand and fight. We will wait for you in Nueviant."

"Nueviant?"

"Yes, it is about twelve kilometers east of our location on this road. I talked with the commander of a SS unit in the village. He has not seen any American units."

"A Waffen SS unit? Maybe they will send help," a junior officer hoped.

"No, it's a Gestapo unit, under a Strumbannführer named Gerickman. I doubt if he'll send any help."

"Just as well, Herr Hauptmann. The Gestapo would sell their own mother's souls to save their own skins."

"Any other questions? If not, get back to your platoons."

The faces of his commanders reflected relief that they were not going to fight to the last man as Hitler had ordered at Stalingrad and El Alamein.

After his commanders headed back to their respective platoons, Dietz stared in the direction of the American lines. To try and hold them indefinitely would only lead to the destruction of his 2nd Company, and that was not going to happen.

Chapter 11

The four men stood looking at the crude layout of the village, which had been drawn by Wallace. Their helmets and automatic weapons had been piled on the hood of the American jeep. Wallace, Weselmann, and Rickett were all smoking cigarettes. Vopel had his familiar pipe, adding to the aroma.

"We need a suitable battle plan for Herr Gerickman's men," said Wallace. "What does Gerickman have in the way of weapons and vehicles?"

"Two armored half-tracks, two kubelwagens, one staff car and about ten trucks. He also has at least two maybe three tripod mounted MG42s," Weselmann replied.

"And how many men does he have?"

"Over a hundred and twenty men, a fifth of them armed with automatic weapons."

"That's a lot of firepower to stop with eighteen men," Rickett sighed, tossing his cigarette to the ground.

"One advantage we have is the combat experience of our men. The Gestapo outnumber us seven to one, but they're garrison troops with little if any combat experience," Weselmann commented.

"Are you sure Gerickman will come back to avenge his brother and risk being captured or killed?" Wallace asked.

Weselmann looked to Vopel. "I would tell them, Franz."

"Tell us what, Sergeant."

"After we killed Otto Gerickman, we searched his staff car for weapons. We didn't find weapons. We found something we weren't looking for," Weselmann replied.

"What did you find?"

"Come. I will show you."

"Where?"

"In the church basement."

The four soldiers entered the church, briefly viewing the damage done by the Gestapo. Weselmann and Vopel then led the Americans down the steps to the small storeroom in back of the basement. Seeing where his men had covered the cases, Weselmann pulled back the tarp revealing the cases taken from the staff car.

"Take a look, Lieutenant."

Wallace opened the first case cautiously, almost as if he was checking out a suspected booby trap. Stuffed with diamonds and precious stones, he moved quickly to the second case, which was full of French francs. Rickett joined in the search opening the last case filled with gold wedding bands and diamond studded earrings. He let out an audible, "Good God."

"But where would Gerickman get all this?" Wallace asked, stunned by the revelation.

"Stolen from deported Jews and other political prisoners is our guess," Vopel surmised.

"Cover them back up. We can turn it over to the proper authorities, after we deal with Gerickman," Wallace said.

"Now you see why he will be back."

"Do all your men know of these cases?" Rickett asked.

"Yes, but none of us want anything to do with this blood money."

"Jerry, I think we'll keep this from our guys unless it becomes necessary. Gold and money bring out the worst in men. I think I know our guys pretty well, but it makes no sense to complicate the situation."

After replacing the tarps, they returned outside to continue planning the coming fight. Looking at their watches, they had about an hour to prepare for the Gestapo.

"Herr Gerickman will probably bring his unit directly to the center of the village. When he arrived yesterday, all the vehicles crowded together, forming a circle around their commander," Weselmann explained.

"We need to emplace the .30 caliber where it can command the center of the village," Wallace said.

Twenty yards from the church were the remains of an old shop evidently destroyed by fire. All that remained was a stone foundation that caught Rickett's eye.

"How about this burned building, Lieutenant? Could conceal the .30 caliber and a few riflemen."

"Works for me, Sergeant. Also deploy the balance of our guys in the north woods to cover that side of the village."

"That leaves the south. Your men will cover that end of the village, Corporal Vopel. You decide where to position your squad."

"And, myself?" Weselmann asked.

"You and I will fight together. Not that I don't trust you but your men would be less likely to change sides if they knew it would cost your life."

"The same would work for your men, Lieutenant."

"That's right. Just call it insurance."

Vopel and Rickett shook their heads, each man worried about this fragile truce.

"Jerry, get our guys into position."

"Hans, setup our defense."

Rickett and Vopel looked at each other then shrugged their shoulders before carrying Wallace's plan.

"We need to deploy our troops to attain their maximum effectiveness. Do you have any sharpshooters among your men?" Wallace asked.

"Private Baake is our best rifle shot, Corporal Rotter isn't as good, but he can hit his target," said Weselmann.

Weselmann had decided to let the American lieutenant command this composite unit. It made perfect logic. Wallace outranked him and had the majority of the men.

"Does either of them speak English?"

"No."

"Goldstein, tell Baumann I need him."

"Have your Private Baake setup with Corporal Baumann, our interpreter, in the church steeple," Wallace suggested, as Weselmann nodded his approval.

Weselmann turned looking towards several of his men gathered at the bakery, yelling "Baake, come here."

"Yes, Sergeant."

Baumann and Baake arrived at the jeep about the same time wondering what their respective leaders wanted.

"This is Corporal Baumann, Karl. You two are going to set up shop in the steeple."

The puzzled trooper looked to Wallace who nodded his head in agreement. Baumann then trotted to the church followed by Baake.

"They looked enthusiastic didn't they," Wallace mused.

"I don't think either of us thought our men would jump for joy, fighting with men who killed close friends, just yesterday," Weselmann replied.

"I know this is a crazy idea, enemies fighting for a common purpose against a truly evil foe," the American lieutenant reflected.

"The odds are that some, maybe most of us will not survive this day," Weselmann replied grimly.

"Let's get a positive attitude, Sergeant. We're not dead yet."

Retrieving their helmets and weapons, the two men went to check the defenses. As they turned they both noticed the small figure of Sister Monique walking to the church. She no longer walked with a spring in her step as she did when she first met Weselmann. For a moment she looked in his direction but continued her journey into the church.

Entering the church the two men could find no trace of the young novice. Weselmann thought she had gone to her private chamber in the basement. He stopped for a moment, he needed to talk to her, but he first needed to be ready for Herr Gerickman.

"Problem, Sergeant."

Weselmann shook his head as he started climbing the spiral stairs to the steeple. The brick steeple had numerous religious paintings attached to the wall. Wallace wondered why the SS left these alone, as they had trashed the church.

At the top of the stairs, the two soldiers sat staring at each other. Each one acknowledged the arrival of Wallace and Weselmann without taking their eyes off his counterpart.

"Baumann, the enemy is out there today, not in here."

Reaching into his pocket his hand reappeared with a candy bar which he broke in half, tossing a piece to Baake and to Baumann.

"Danke, Leutnant"

"Thanks, sir."

"Now while you two are chewing on one of my prized possessions, listen up."

Weselmann translated Wallace's comments to Baake. Both soldiers broke into a grin.

"When the last truck pulls into the center of the town, shoot the driver. If you can't see him, fire through the cab of the vehicle. That'll be our signal to open up. Think of it this way; together we can get out of here to live another day." Wallace explained.

Wallace and Weselmann then exited the steeple.

At the base of the stairs Weselmann said, "Too bad, you had to give up your last candy bar."

Wallace's hand disappeared, into his jacket, and then reappeared with another candy bar, breaking it in two giving one piece to Weselmann, "Who said it was my last candy bar?" he said, smiling.

Wallace, checking his watch, calculated the Gestapo should be arriving in about fifteen to twenty minutes. Vopel and Rickett had signaled that their men were ready and emplaced.

"Well, we've done everything we can, but surprise is the key. If we hit them hard before they can set a defense, we'll be all right," Wallace hoped.

"What about the half-tracks?" Weselmann asked.

"Well if he comes back like he arrived the first time, all the vehicles bunched together, they won't be able to maneuver. Should be able to knock them out fairly easy. Are these the enclosed type with a turret or open troop carriers?" Wallace asked.

"They're troop carriers with a shield mounted MG42 and a removable MG34 in an anti-aircraft mount."

"Good, then they can be knocked out with grenades," Wallace replied.

"Unless Herr Gerickman splits his force, we should have a good chance of success."

"Splits his force?"

Wallace let out an audible sigh at the thought of having to defend against two units with eighteen men.

"What is it?"

"Nothing, let's find a place to greet Herr Gerickman."

They found a couple of logs thrown together that made a good hiding place. Wallace took one last look at his defenses before lying down behind the logs.

"Lieutenant!" Rickett shouted.

Wallace looked to Rickett who pointed to the church steeple. Leaning out of the top window in the steeple, Baumann was pointing to the east. The show was on.

Chapter 12

Wallace and Weselmann's men took cover when the rumble of the SS vehicles approaching the village disturbed the afternoon tranquility. The fifteen Gestapo men could be seen riding in a truck and a kubelwagen. The SS men didn't seem to have any concerns as they rode in the vehicles with their weapons slung across their backs. Wallace was amazed that they were riding into town like it was a parade unaware that death was about to greet them. Combat troops would never enter a town in enemy country like they were on leave. Evidently the SS Major didn't think he needed more than this many to handle the seven panzer grenadiers.

"The Gestapo isn't taking you and your men very serious. Looks like they're going on holiday," Wallace whispered.

"They're used to intimidating and pushing around civilians. I can imagine they expect us to surrender and willfully stand against a wall to be shot," replied Weselmann. "They think that the mere sight of their black uniforms alone will cause us to give up."

"Your men will fight, won't they Sergeant?"

"I told you earlier how my men feel towards the Gestapo. We fear and hate them almost as much as the French do. They have the power of life and death over not only us but our families as well. It is to our advantage that none of the SS survive this day. My men will fight and will kill as many as possible for our families' lives are at stake."

The two men raised their weapons as the vehicles came to a halt in the center of the village. An SS lieutenant stood up in the kubelwagen and shouted an order seconds before a rifle cracked.

The shot shattered the windshield of the truck, killing the driver. At the sound of the shot, the machine gun crew opened up on the disembarking Gestapo men. Like the civilians that they massacred in the past, the SS tried to outrun the .30 caliber rounds that ripped and shredded their bodies. The well emplaced members of German-American unit picked off the fleeing SS. Some of the SS returned fire but were quickly reduced to bloody corpses on the ground. The Gestapo that found the cover of the truck were cut down from behind by Wallace's men in the woods.

The SS lieutenant tumbled out the kubelwagen hit by the combined fire of Wallace and Weselmann as his driver spun the scout car around amid the hail of fire.

"Glassman, nail that scout car!" Wallace yelled.

The gunner swiveled his Browning machine gun too late to stop the speeding vehicle from reaching its goal. The scout car was hit several times, but the driver skillfully evaded the carnage around the truck as he sped out of the village.

The firefight lasted less than five minutes, ending in the death of fourteen black-clad men lying in and around the truck. Wallace and Weselmann walked to the fallen SS checking for any sign of life.

"Goldstein, collect their weapons and ammo belts," Wallace ordered.

"What do you want me to do with them, Lieutenant?

"Take them to the church and put them in the storeroom."

"Any casualties?" Wallace asked

"One of the Germans took a round in the leg," Rickett reported, "Stazinski is tending to him. I think his name is Pinket or something like that."

"Private Piontek. Excuse me, I will check on my man, Lieutenant," said Weselmann, leaving for the church.

"How's the ammo?" Wallace asked.

"Weselmann's men can replenish what they expended from the dead Gestapo and might even gain a little extra. Our guys used about fifteen percent of rifle ammo and we're down to four belts for the Browning.

"Any of our Germans a problem?" Wallace asked.

"No, not counting Glassman's crew, they dropped more SS than we did. They're a tough squad of veterans," Rickett replied.

"That kraut in the scout car got away. The next fight won't be quite the cakewalk. They won't be surprised like this bunch," said Wallace, looking at the dead Germans in the road. "Herr Major will send his half-tracks in first then the men. There are still more than a hundred Gestapo men left in Gerickman's unit. At least the odds are better than ten minutes ago."

"Maybe the krauts will give it up and head for the safety of Strasbourg?" Rickett asked.

"I don't think so. We've got greed and revenge working here. Gerickman wants two things: Weselmann and his men dead and wants the hidden loot from his brother's staff car. He might give it up instead of revenging his brother's death, but he wants the gold and jewels hidden in that vehicle."

"Well I hope you're wrong, Lieutenant. But the more you think about it, it makes more sense than us fighting with Weselmann against Gerickman," Rickett said, shaking his head.

"Get some of our men to load the dead Gestapo in the truck and move it out of the way."

"Right, Lieutenant."

Wallace watched the soldiers of two nations loading SS bodies into the truck, thinking he's right this doesn't make any sense.

Corporal Vopel was waiting at the entrance of the church when Weselmann arrived, "How did Piontek get wounded?"

"One of the SS, who seemed to have some combat experience, dropped to the ground as soon as the shooting started. He was able to fire a full clip before he was killed. The youngster stood up to get a better look when he was hit above his right knee. He should be all right."

Weselmann entered the church in time to see the American medic give Piontek a cigarette. Piontek didn't speak any English, but the medic spoke to him in a way that seemed to ease his suffering. These Americans fought and killed with great efficiency in battle but had unusual compassion for a wounded enemy. Weselmann could only admire them and the nation that produced these soldiers.

"How is he, doctor?"

"He'll be all right. The slug went clean through without doing any permanent damage. Once the morphine wears off, he'll be sore as hell, but in a week should be good as new," replied Stazinski as he lightly slapped the young panzer grenadier on the back.

"Thank you, doctor."

"*Danke, Doktor*," Piontek added.

Stazinski smiled as he walked outside to see if anyone else was hurt in the firefight.

A smiling Weselmann asked Piontek without expecting an answer, "Didn't I teach you better than to stand up in combat?"

"Sergeant, what happens if we survive the SS assault? I like these Americans. How can we go back to trying to kill them?" Piontek asked.

Weselmann's smile disappeared. "Because they will try to kill you; that's the nature of war. It is best not to know your enemy personally. Just shoot the uniform and keep the man in it faceless. Don't worry the American lieutenant and I will work something out when we defeat the Gestapo." The optimism in his voice was as much for his own benefit as well as Piontek's.

"Yes Sergeant, I feel relieved as well,"

Weselmann turned to a broadly smiling Corporal Vopel who evidently had been listening.

"Corporal Vopel, don't you have something to do outside?" Weselmann replied, trying not to smile.

"I will check the men, Sergeant," Vopel said, crisply saluting. He turned, gave a wink to Weselmann, and then exited the church.

"Piontek, I want you to stay off that leg. I'll let you know if we need you. Have you seen Sister Monique?"

"Yes, I saw her in the sanctuary."

Weselmann took off his helmet and laid down his Schmeisser in the last pew. Sister Monique was kneeling in the first row of pews softly praying. She wore a gray skirt and white blouse with a blue scarf covering her short brown hair. As he walked towards her, he saw the tears that streamed down her face.

"Sister, can I do something for you?"

"No, I'm asking God's forgiveness for the trouble I have caused."

"It is not your fault that Hauptsturmführer . . ." Weselmann stopped himself, not wanting to refresh her memory of the events.

"No, I have forgiven him for what he did to me. It is all the young men who have and will die because of what happened. I feel responsible for their deaths," she softly sobbed. "And now I feel that because of what happened, I can no longer become a nun. I say I have forgiven him but part of me still hates him."

"It is not you who killed Otto Gerickman and his men. If anyone needs forgiveness from God it is myself. Had I not killed him, he would be half way to Strasbourg, and I would be trying to rejoin my company, Sister," Weselmann reflected.

She stood up before him saying softly, "Please call me Michelle, Sergeant."

He answered, "Franz, my first name is Franz."

Weselmann took the handkerchief from her hand wiping the tears away. "No matter how this ends, none of this was your fault."

She slipped her hand into his. They looked into each other's eyes for what seemed like an eternity when Corporal Vopel entered yelling.

"Franz, where are you? The American lieutenant wants you."

Weselmann chuckled softly to Michelle, "He knows my first name too."

"Tell him I'm on my way," Weselmann answered.

"Please stay in the church basement until the fighting is over," Weselmann pleaded.

"I will. You are a good man Franz. Please be careful."

He nodded to her then retrieved his helmet and Schmeisser before exiting the church.

Wallace and Rickett were discussing the best way to defend the village when Weselmann and Vopel joined them.

"How is your man, Piontek?"

"He will recover, Lieutenant."

"Good."

"How do you think Gerickman will attack us?" Wallace asked.

"Since he knows that more than seven men hold the village, he will have several scouts sent to see our positions and gauge our strength before the assault." Weselmann replied.

"What would you do to mislead the scouts?"

"I would allow them to observe only some of our men setting up defensive positions at the far end of the village. The rest would be hidden in the church, these houses and the woods at the north side of the village. If he proceeds to the west end of the village to attack the machine gun position, we have a killing ground setup with crossfire from the west and north."

"What about this high ground to the south behind the church? If he sets up his heavy machine guns up there, he can control the whole village," Rickett reminded them.

"Jerry, how many men will it take to keep the Gestapo off this hill?"

"Give me Glassman's crew and two men. We'll keep them off the hill and cover the village as well." Rickett replied.

"We can set up a couple fake machine gun positions using old pipes from the houses. From a distance they would look like the real thing. What do you think Sergeant Weselmann? Will this fool Gerickman?"

"Gerickman is no fool, but if we keep the balance of the men hidden, it should work."

"We do have a big advantage or as you Americans say, an ace in the hole," added Vopel.

"If the SS man who got away didn't notice our uniforms during the ambush, we could be a big surprise to them. Imagine if American soldiers burst out of the woods on your flank during a battle. Would you think they were another unit or the enemy? Even if they did figure it out, most would be dead before they could react."

"Ace in the hole? Where did you learn that lingo, Corporal?" Wallace asked.

"My uncle left Germany in 1933 and now lives in Hannibal, Missouri. Before the war, he would write my father telling him of American customs and slang. I would like to visit your country when this war is over."

"Well Corporal if your idea works, when I get back to the good old USA, you can come visit."

"Sergeant Weselmann, take your squad and conceal yourselves in the north woods."

"Well gentlemen, that's the plan. Let's do it."

Weselmann and Vopel moved off to collect their men, while Rickett and Wallace discussed how to deploy their squad members.

"Sandy, move the .30 caliber to the hilltop behind the church and take whatever men you need for support."

"Do you think the plan will work?" Rickett asked.

"Well I remember in military history in ROTC, back in college, that confederate troops dressed in blue uniforms caught the union troops off guard at the battle of Bull Run during the civil war. It helped to produce a southern victory," Wallace replied.

"You mean Manassas Junction, don't you, Lieutenant? That's what we called it down south."

"Whatever it was called, the uniforms gave the edge to the victors."

"What if the Germans change sides?" asked Rickett.

"I don't think they will, but you'll be looking down their throats with the Browning on the high ground. If they do, don't hesitate. Cut them down."

"Killing Germans was a lot simpler when they were a faceless enemy."

"I know. Get the men moving, Jerry."

As Rickett walked away, Wallace watched the German non-coms briefing their men thinking to himself how these seemingly likable men can support such a devil like Hitler and his gang. He wiped the thoughts from his mind. Can't think about that now. Have to concentrate on fighting our way through the SS to get back to our lines.

His thoughts were interrupted by the sounds of muffled gunfire at the roadblock to the west. Maybe our guys will breakthrough and all bets would be off; it was a possibility. One thing was for sure. This mission was getting crazier by the minute.

Chapter 13

Gestapo man Ernest Meier was minutes away from reporting what happened to Lieutenant Kleist's unit. For the second time, he had seen all his comrades killed in a matter of minutes. How would his commander take the news this time? He had thought of deserting, but where would he go. He couldn't go back to Nueviant where sudden death waited for anyone wearing a Gestapo uniform. He had to put his fate in Herr Gerickman's hands. How could he explain surviving two encounters with those deadly panzer grenadiers, or were they? He thought he saw American soldiers as well as Wehrmacht troops, but that didn't make sense. Everything happened so fast he could have imagined it.

His bullet riddled kubelwagen skidded to a halt, throwing up a cloud of dust, as Kurt Gerickman and his officers gathered to hear his report.

Seeing only the scout car returning again, Gerickman slowly and in a controlled voice asked the SS man, "Did Lieutenant Kleist carry out my orders?"

In that instant, SS Gestapo man Ernest Meier decided to gamble his life. He came close to death last time when he told of the death of his comrades to Gerickman. He decided to lie.

"He sent me to get help, sir. He is fighting with the Wehrmacht soldiers in the village," blurted Meier nervously.

Gerickman glanced at the scout car before asking his next question, "Is Lieutenant Kleist wounded?"

"I don't know sir. He was fine when I left him. Shouldn't we hurry, he needs our help," Meier pleaded.

Gerickman leaned in and dragged the hapless man out of the kubelwagen by his collar. He shoved Meier face down into the passenger side. "Then whose blood is this?" Gerickman yelled.

Unable to come up with the proper answer, Meier stood speechless as Gerickman slapped the man hard enough to draw blood, knocking him against the door of the scout car.

"I ask you again. Did Kleist carry out my orders?" Gerickman demanded.

"No, sir. He and the rest were killed as we entered the town."

"And you alone survived to tell me what happened. I can barely condone a coward, but I will not condone a lying coward," said Gerickman, drawing his Luger from his holster.

Meier started to reply as the first shot sliced through his jugular vein. Grabbing for his throat, he thought Herr Gerickman should know of the extra troops in the village. Strange, he thought, thinking of that as he was dying. The second shot entered above his left eye. As fragments of bone and blood splattered the kubelwagen, all his thoughts came to an end.

Looking with disdain at the dead man at his feet, Gerickman replaced the Luger to his holster. His officers had seen many civilians slaughtered without emotion, but Meier was one of their own. Several became ill at the execution that took place. Noticing their discomfort at his actions, Gerickman began shouting orders, "Assemble the men, we are all going back to Nueviant. Now!"

Junior officers shouted orders as the men scrambled to retrieve their equipment, before gathering near their vehicles. Gerickman walked to the two half-tracks parked at the far end of the village.

"Mueller. Zimwalt."

"Yes, Herr Gerickman," the two half-track commanders replied.

"I don't want your vehicles ambushed, move to the rear of the column. If we encounter trouble come up fast in support, but do not engage in close combat. Is that understood?"

"Jahowl, Herr Strumbannführer."

"We leave in ten minutes. Have your crews ready," said Gerickman, walking to the knot of officers gathered at his staff car. He noticed the look of fear in his officers' eyes.

"Sir, is it worth risking our lives to get Weselmann and his men? What about the Americans?" SS Lieutenant Karl Fleischer asked.

"The Americans are being held up by Dietz's unit. They have killed over twenty of our comrades. We can not run away from that. We have time to deal with Weselmann and his men."

He couldn't tell his real reason to go back. The last thing he wanted to do was go back to Nueviant, but there was a score to settle and a staff car to recover. He knew he couldn't bring Otto back but those treasure cases were his. Nothing was going to get in his way to retrieve them; not Weselmann or the Americans.

"We must have a plan, sir. They have shot up two of our units. We could make it three if we ride in without a plan," one of the officers said.

"Quite right, Lieber. We will drive within a kilometer of the village. We will wait while a squad of men under Unterstrumführer Ludwig will scout the village to see how Weselmann is deployed in Nueviant. I can't believe he and his scum killed Kleist's men so easy. He must have had some help, but who?"

"Dietz?" Lieber asked.

"I don't think so. He wanted me to send troops to him, because he thought we were Waffen SS. I got the impression from him he would hold until his ammunition ran out," Gerickman replied, considering the unknown situation.

Two SS men carried the earthly remains of Ernest Meier past the officers, placing him next to the café. Gerickman saw the disdain in the eyes of the men who carried Meier out of the road.

"Perhaps, I was too quick in dispatching Meier. He was the only one who could tell us for sure who is in the village. It doesn't matter. After we get Ludwig's report, we'll know who is left."

"What about Klinemann? He needs medical attention as soon as possible," a tall lanky officer named Reppmann asked.

"Klinemann?"

"The cyclist who was wounded yesterday, sir."

"Oh yes. He will have to wait until we deal with Weselmann."

"He can't wait. If we don't get him to a doctor in the next day, he will probably die," Reppmann implored.

The Gestapo treated others with contempt but did take care of their own. To allow the death of a fellow SS man, due to an unpopular order, could cause a mutiny. With the exception of his brother and Bauer, Gerickman had few friends amongst his men. He was running out of people he could trust.

"Very well, inform Private Rauser to take Klinemann to the closest field hospital he can find. We won't need his motorcycle until after we accomplish our task in Nueviant. He can strap a stretcher to his sidecar," Gerickman said, using a reassuring tone.

"Yes, sir."

"We move out in five minutes."

Orders were given as the SS men boarded their vehicles. Soon the village reverberated with the sound of the vehicles revving their engines. The column formed with the late Private Meier's kubelwagen in front and the two half-tracks bringing up the rear.

The afternoon sun was beating down on Gerickman as he gave the signal to move out to the driver of the scout car with Liebig as his passenger. Seeing that all the vehicles were ready to go, Gerickman climbed aboard his staff car as his driver pulled into the flow of the column.

The half-track with the inscription *Heidi*, and its newly applied camouflage of tree branches, was the last vehicle in the column. As a precaution, all the drivers had camouflaged their individual vehicles the best they could to prevent aircraft from spotting their movement.

"I think Gerickman is losing his mind," insisted Guenther Schneider, removing his helmet as the column picked up speed.

"There has to be more than revenge for him to risk his life," Heinz Mueller said, shifting the half-track into second gear.

"This brotherly love stuff is getting old. He's going to get us all killed because of his brother. And I never did like that twit Otto Gerickman."

"You're still upset that he stole your girlfriend Denise. Face it, you are a private, and he is or was a Hauptsturmführer. Rank always turns the pretty girl's head," Mueller said, swerving the half-track to miss a rotting log in the road. A banging on the armored cab told Private Goehl's displeasure at being tossed around in the back of the half-track.

"He gets the girl pregnant and then her old man shoots his daughter for sleeping with a German. Why shoot the girl? He should have shot Gerickman," Schneider said, ignoring his companion in the back.

"Wouldn't have mattered. Our commander would have killed the father, the daughter and the whole family as an example for shooting a German officer. Tonight we'll find out what is going on when we check our commander's staff car."

"Heinz, just be sure you don't end up like Meier."

"Meier was a weakling, I always wondered how he got in the Gestapo," Mueller scoffed, grinding the gears into third.

"Herr Gerickman is not to be fooled with. The man is dangerous."

"Guenther," Mueller replied, looking at his passenger with a sinister look. "I am dangerous."

Chapter 14

Weselmann and Vopel looked to the sky, in the general direction of the roadblock, as they heard the drone of planes. They recognized the hated Jabos, the German nickname for American P-47 fighter-bombers. At first the planes headed directly for the village then made a sweeping turn, using the west road as a landmark to help locate the roadblock. A few minutes later the sounds of a bombing run echoed in the village.

"They're hitting Hauptmann Dietz's position again. The artillery we heard earlier must not have succeeded," Vopel concluded.

"Well, at least it means he's holding the roadblock," replied Weselmann.

"Yes, but for how long? Our American friends will only help us until somebody else arrives in this village, besides Herr Gerickman's men. Have you given some thought to the notion of what to do when we defeat the Gestapo?" Hans asked, looking somber.

Weselmann scanned the village trying to determine if any gun pits needed a bit more camouflage, when he saw Baake's signal from the church steeple.

"We can worry about that later. Karl has seen something. Get our men ready to assemble in the woods," said Weselmann, trotting to the church where Lieutenant Wallace was receiving the news from Baumann.

"Baumann and your man Baake spotted some activity about a kilometer and a half on the east road. Whoever it is, they're not doing a good job of sneaking around," Wallace said.

"Probably Herr Gerickman, his men aren't line soldiers. Most of them have never fired their weapons while someone was shooting back." Weselmann replied.

"Then they'll make mistakes, which will work to our advantage. Could you see Rickman's position from where you were?"

"No, it's well hidden. If not for seeing where they dug in, I wouldn't know its location."

"But being a veteran, you'd be a little apprehensive that something was up there. Wouldn't you, Sergeant?"

"If I was ordered to defend this village, I would do exactly what you are doing. Unless Herr Gerickman has some former Waffen SS amongst his men to advise him, he may not think about it."

"How's your ammunition?"

"We have enough."

"Grenades."

"About fifteen. Found some in the Gestapo trucks."

"I want to leave your man Baake in the steeple with Baumann."

"Baumann, barricade the church doors from the inside. We don't want Gerickman's men to get inside and turn the church into a fort. Then join Baake back in the steeple."

Baumann trotted back into the church with a little more enthusiasm than the first time he was teamed with Baake.

He saw his medic exiting the church. "Doc, you and Piontek stay in the church. Grab one of the German weapons, just in case."

"Still don't trust me completely, Lieutenant?" Weselmann mused.

"The last thing I want to do is turn my weapon on you, Weselmann. But you are an enemy soldier, and my first responsibility is to my men. Pausing for a moment, Wallace continued, "With a couple of your men in the church, I feel that the truce will hold until we deal with Gerickman. After that, I hope we can work something out."

"What is the signal for us to attack?" Weselmann asked.

"I leave that to you. You'll know when to hit them. If possible, take out their half-tracks with your grenades."

Wallace checked his watch. "I figure we have ten minutes. Take your men into the north woods. Good luck," said Wallace, thinking if all the Germans were as competent as Weselmann, his unit would have suffered a lot more casualties to this point.

Weselmann nodded. He started to trot away then stopped, giving Wallace a salute. "Good luck to you, Lieutenant."

Wallace returned the salute, picking up his Thompson and binoculars then headed for the far end of the village, where the fake strongpoint was setup. Lepper, Goldstein and Jenkins looked uneasy as their lieutenant plopped down alongside them, behind hasty thrown up defenses.

"What're our chances, Lieutenant?" Goldstein asked, setting his grenades on the lip of his makeshift dugout.

"Well if everything goes as we hope and pray, we'll be OK," Wallace replied.

"Our so-called allies did fine in the first fight, but will they back us up if our lives are on the line?" Jenkins asked.

"If the chips don't look good for us, I bet they change sides," Goldstein declared with disdain.

"If they do, Sergeant Rickman, with the .30 caliber, has orders to kill Weselmann and his men first. But you ought to have more confidence in your leader's judgment, Goldstein."

"I trust him, sir," Lepper said. "When we first met under the flag of truce, he didn't seem arrogant like that wounded kraut officer we captured a few weeks back near Metz. Remember, Lieutenant."

"Oh yes, Oberleutnant Kurt Getz. He wouldn't let Stazinski check his wound until he knew he wasn't Jewish. Kept spouting that trash about the master race," Wallace laughed, along with Goldstein and Lepper.

"I don't get it, sir. What's so funny?" Jenkins asked.

"That's right. You didn't join the unit until after that happened," Wallace said, still smiling.

"Are you going to tell me or what?"

"Tell him, Goldstein."

"After Stazinski gave him some plasma, I said you didn't give him that blood. The kraut said what blood? And I," Goldstein paused laughing before continuing, "told him that was special blood for American soldiers of Jewish descent only. You know what that does to your facial features if you're not Jewish. He goes as white as a sheet, demanding another transfusion with non-Jewish blood. He didn't get it, and we never did tell him the truth," Goldstein snickered as this time all four soldiers broke into laughter.

"Ok, hold it down. They will be here in another five to ten minutes. We want them to notice us, but not make them too overconfident. I think Weselmann and his men will do fine. Got a good feeling about him."

Wallace and his men checked their weapons placing extra clips in easy reach. Four minutes later, it was near 4:00 when Baumann signaled to Wallace, pointing to the east end of the dirt road. Two black-clad soldiers hugged the tree line on either side of the dirt, trying not to be seen by anyone in the village. When they were satisfied that the street was deserted, they signaled the balance of their recon unit to proceed. Ten Gestapo men slowly advanced towards the opposite end of the village where Wallace's men waited, peering through the openings in the rubble.

"Remember, none of them get in the church," Wallace whispered.

"What if they try to flank us on the left?" Goldstein whispered back.

"Weselmann's squad will cover our flank."

"Yeah, I'll believe that when I see it, that is, if I'm still alive," Goldstein quipped.

The German scout leader stopped about thirty yards from their position, near the center of the village, before raising his binoculars. Slowly he scanned the village looking for any sign of life, while several of his men checked the houses at their end of the village. His men looked nervous expecting to suffer the same fate as their comrades at any moment.

"Lepper take off your helmet and raise it just above the edge of the rubble with that piece of pipe by your side," Wallace whispered.

Seeing the movement, the German non-com stopped briefly centering on Lepper's helmet. Instead of ordering his men to take cover or attack, he acted indifferent to the apparent presence of enemy forces; instead he signaled them to withdraw. Soon they were back out of sight down the east road.

"What gives, Lieutenant? They had to see Lepper's helmet. Why didn't they hit us to gauge our strength?" Jenkins asked.

"They will, but where and how? There are over a hundred of them, with light armored support and only sixteen of us, they could hit us from several locations."

The silence was broken by the sounds of grenades and automatic fire coming from the direction of the hilltop behind the church, followed by sounds of the machine gun joining the fray.

"They're hitting Sarge's position. Do we send help, Lieutenant?" Goldstein blurted.

"No, he has the .30 caliber sweeping the hill. He'll be OK, but—," Wallace's reply was broke off by the sounds of the squeaking tracks of a half-track heading their way. It broke out of the woods followed by about two dozen black-clad Gestapo men.

"Here they come! Aim for the driver's view slit."

Wallace and the men fired until driven to the ground by the heavy volume of fire from the heavy machine gun mounted on top of the vehicle's cab, protected by an armored shield. Hit by rifle fire from the steeple and several GIs, hidden on Wallace's right flank, four SS men spun to the ground. As anticipated the remaining Germans tried a flanking movement to the left, while the half-track's MG42 kept Wallace's men pinned down.

"Where's that kraut, Weselmann?" Goldstein screamed, as the half-track moved closer to his position.

"Wish I knew," Wallace yelled, as the round after round smacked into the stone foundation of the old house.

"Sir, we can't stay here!"

"They'll be on us in another minute!"

"All right, get ready to move!" Wallace shouted, thinking *I should never have trusted a German.*

Seconds before giving the order to move, the half-track burst into flames, destroyed by several stick grenades. The Gestapo men spun around in panic to find the new threat, first relieved the troops were German, and then dismayed as Weselmann's panzer grenadiers poured deadly accurate fire into their ranks. No longer pinned down, Wallace and his men helped finish the almost helpless Gestapo men, who were caught in the inescapable crossfire.

After finishing off the Gestapo at the burning half-track, Weselmann and his men ran, jumping in with Wallace and his men. All the firing had stopped in the village, not a live Gestapo man was left in Nueviant.

"Had us worried but nice work, Sergeant Weselmann?" Wallace said, truly relieved.

"Had to wait until the half-track turned before tossing in the grenades."

"See Lieutenant, I told you. You had nothing to worry about," Goldstein remarked.

Wallace didn't say a word, just smiled at the young soldier.

"Any of your men hurt?" Wallace asked looking at the tired faces of German soldiers lying around, before realizing everyone was fine except Vopel who received a very slight arm wound.

"Lieutenant."

"Yes, Corporal Vopel."

"I would like to know. Do I receive another cluster on my German wound badge or one of your Purple Hearts?"

"I'll take that under consideration," Wallace smiled.

"Thank you," the impish corporal beamed.

"Jenkins get over to the hilltop. Tell Rickett I want to see him. Stay there until somebody relieves you."

Wallace and Weselmann climbed out of the foundation, standing side by side staring at their handiwork. Surrounded by Gestapo bodies, the half-track burned brightly, the tree branches used for camouflage fueled the fire, which was slowly incinerating anything flammable, which included its human crew. Both men had that grim look of combat soldiers who didn't like killing but knew it was a job to be done. The moment was broken by the arrival of Wallace's top sergeant.

"How bad did we get hurt?" Wallace asked. It was a question he always dreaded the answer.

"Perry got hit in the left shoulder. Doc's bandaging him now in the church. He should be okay but we need to get him to a dressing station in the next few days."

"Anybody else?"

"Billings got nicked on the leg, but he can still fight."

"Doesn't sound too bad."

Rickett looked around at the milling soldiers, content that all were well. "I thought you guys were a goner."

"Our plan worked pretty well, except I've lost ten years of my life. But our German allies came to the rescue."

"I know. We could see everything from our position after Gerickman's men withdrew. Your men did a number on that SS half-track," an impressed Rickett said.

"The Gestapo were slow to return fire because of our uniforms. We weren't. We had as you say an edge," Weselmann replied.

"How did it all start at the hilltop?" Wallace asked.

"Gerickman sent two squads and a MG42 to the hilltop by way of an old deer trail. They tried to be quiet, but they sounded like a couple of bull elephants. They didn't even scout the hill, just walked up like it was a Sunday field trip."

"Garrison troops," Weselmann said, shaking his head.

"Yeah," Rickett said, acknowledging Weselmann's comment with a nod, "Held our fire until we couldn't miss, then we let them have it."

"Did you capture that machine gun?" Wallace asked, hoping they could add its firepower.

"We have it, but a grenade went off next to its firing mechanism. It's just a piece of useless iron now."

"At least they can't use it against us, anymore. Check the guys for ammo. Corporal Vopel will see to your men and get a weapons' check as well."

Both men nodded and left, leaving the two commanders alone.

Wallace removed his helmet, and leaned his Thompson against the foundation wall. After running his hand through his hair, he sat on the edge of the foundation, keeping a watchful eye on the east road. Producing his diminishing pack of cigarettes, he took one before flipping the pack to Weselmann. The German sergeant took one then after an approving nod from Wallace, passed the pack around to the Germans and Americans who had fought together. When the pack was returned, only two cigarettes were left. Returning it to Wallace, he then sat alongside him letting his own helmet fall to the ground, keeping his MP40 in his lap.

"We were lucky this time. They did about everything we thought they would except they first attacked Rickett's position. Without the fire support of the .30 caliber, I didn't know if we could hold them. But like the cavalry, you arrived in the nick of time," Wallace said.

"Have you noticed what's missing from the village?"

Looking around Wallace saw what his companion meant. "The staff car is gone."

"We noticed from the woods as soon as the car exited so did the rest of Gerickman's men. He sacrificed these men not for my head but for the valuables that were hidden in that car. They were nothing more than a diversion for Herr Gerickman's greed," an angry Weselmann said, staring at the unfortunate dead men around the burning half-track.

"Then since he has realized by now that what he wants isn't in the staff car, I envisage that he is one unhappy SS major, Herr Weselmann."

"I believe you are correct, Lieutenant," a satisfied sergeant replied, thinking of Herr Gerickman's displeasure.

"I wonder what he'll do next? Check that, I know what he's going to do," Wallace said pointing to the road, where three SS men stood with a white flag.

Wallace and Weselmann quickly retrieved their helmets and weapons as Rickett trotted to them.

"Look Franz, Herr Gerickman wants to surrender," Vopel quipped.

"I don't believe surrender is on his mind, Hans," Weselmann replied.

Looking through his binoculars for any other movement, Wallace said, "Shall we let Herr Gerickman stew for a while?"

"I don't think we can. Looks like he's coming to us, Lieutenant," Rickett said, flipping the safety off on his Thompson.

"Remember Lieutenant, you can't trust this man," Vopel stated the obvious.

"I have no intention of trusting him. You can't trust Germans," Wallace replied, giving his panzer grenadier companions a sheepish grin.

Chapter 15

Kurt Gerickman and two of his officers, in their immaculate black uniforms, walked stiffly towards the tired, dirty looking veterans. Kurt Gerickman knew his men weren't combat troops, but he had hoped for a better showing. All he had to show for the last attack was the loss of twenty-seven men and a half-track for an empty staff car. Instead of Weselmann's head and the return of his possessions, he had seen his men slaughtered like cattle. And now he was forced to negotiate with his brother's killers, it was almost too much to bear.

In the early evening light, it was difficult to see details of his adversary's uniforms. As he advanced closer, he confirmed the unbelievable. It's true, Americans and Germans fighting together. That's impossible. How did Weselmann talk them into helping him? When the survivors returned saying they were fighting together, I dismissed it as a hallucination. But there they are standing side by side. Gerickman motioned his companions to stay back, as he advanced the last 50 feet to the four men.

"That's far enough, Herr Gerickman. What can I do for you?"

"You have me at a disadvantage, you are?"

"Lieutenant Wallace."

The haughty SS major tried a poor attempt at intimidation. "I will make this brief. You will at once hand over my brother's killers and any possessions taken from his car or suffer the consequences."

"What consequences are those?"

"We will attack until you and your men are dead. I take no prisoners," said Gerickman, hoping this American would be frightened by his tone and determination.

"And your brother's killers, who would they be?"

"The treacherous scum who murdered my brother stand next to you," said Gerickman, looking with total disdain at Weselmann and Vopel. "They are not only traitors to the Führer but murdered an innocent Gestapo officer and his men in course of their duties."

"Innocent men do not murder and rape nuns," Wallace angrily replied.

"How do you know that my brother Otto did these things?" Gerickman asked.

"Sergeant Weselmann told us what happened."

"And you take the word of this worthless sergeant over that of an officer of the Third Reich. These men have no honor. They have betrayed the Führer and Germany. They killed my brother to gain the valuables he carried in his staff car, not because of an indiscretion with a prostitute posing as a nun."

Weselmann's face flushed with anger as he took a step towards Gerickman before Wallace stopped him with a hand on his shoulder. "I'll handle this, Sergeant."

"You see the mere mention of the truth, and this scum of a traitor shows his true colors," Gerickman said arrogantly.

"You Nazis are incredible. According to you, only the Nazi elite are worth anything. Raping or murdering a nun is an indiscretion? I believe Weselmann and his men are honorable. He showed us what was in that car and where it is hidden. He wants it returned to its rightful owners, as do I. The only scum here was your brother, or do I put you in that category as well, Herr Gerickman," Wallace retorted disgustedly.

"How dare you speak of my brother that way. You will turn over Weselmann and my possessions. Now!" Gerickman squealed, his hand slipping down to his holster.

I wouldn't," Rickett said, leveling his weapon at Gerickman's gut.

"You have sixty seconds to get out of this village or we open fire, white flag or no white flag, Wallace calmly said, leveling his Thompson at Gerickman's midsection. "Come back into this village, I guarantee you will join your brother."

"You can not—"

"Fifty-five seconds."

Seeing the hopelessness of his situation, Gerickman and his aides hurried out of the village as fast as they could. One of the officers fell face down into the dirt of the road after stumbling over a piece of discarded equipment. Quickly righting himself, the embarrassed officer ran to catch up with his commander who had disappeared into the woods at the east end of the village. The antics of the officer were found very humorous to the four veterans.

"Nicely done, Lieutenant. I liked seeing you put him in his place," a smiling Rickett remarked.

"How's our ammo?"

"Not good. Only two more belts for the .30 caliber. Down to forty percent of M1 ammo or about three clips for each man," replied Rickett.

"About fifty percent left, but we picked up a few rounds from the dead Gestapo," Vopel said.

"Just a few rounds?"

"Same thing at the hilltop. The ones we killed had only one spare clip in their cartridge belts. Even the MG42 gun crew had only one belt," Rickett replied.

"Maybe they're low on ammo," Wallace speculated.

"No, they're not low on ammunition. I saw at least two trucks with ammunition boxes both for their MG42s and small arms," Vopel replied.

"Then the man is sacrificing his own men to run us out of ammo," an incredulous Rickett said.

"And he's not allowing his men much more than what's in their weapons to make sure we don't replenish our supply from the men we kill," Weselmann added.

"Then he'll keep attacking until he gets what he wants or he runs out of men. Its World War I tactics, trading lives for a very small gain," Wallace said, shaking his head.

"Won't his men wise up that he's sacrificing them for personal gain?" Rickett asked.

"They're probably already wondering what Herr Gerickman is doing, but they will follow orders or risk being shot for disobeying. The Gestapo has a knack for killing regardless of the reason. Of course, there is always the chance some may question or even take some action against him," Weselmann said.

"Unfortunately, we can't count on that," Wallace said, handing his Thompson and his extra clips to Rickett. "There are several MP40s in the church. I'll use one of those. Pass out the spare German weapons and ammo to our guys. Tell them only to fire at a sure target. Set sentries for the night"

"Weselmann, come along with me to the church. I need a crash course on the MP40."

The two men walked towards the church, their gaze fixed on the remains of Gerickman's last attack. Night was slowly taking over the daylight as the dying fire of the burnt half-track lit a portion of the village. The Gestapo dead seemed alive in the eerie light of the burning vehicle.

"It'll be dark in about another fifteen minutes. Do you think Gerickman will launch another attack before morning?"

There was silence from Weselmann who stopped to stare at the carnage he helped create.

"Sergeant?"

"They were the hated Gestapo, but they had German mothers and fathers, sisters and brothers, who will mourn for them. What a waste of men. This war has gone on too long, but how to stop the madness?"

"Until one side wins, it will go on. For now we have only to win our own private war to get as many of our men back to our lines as possible."

"Of course, you're right, Lieutenant. A night attack, I don't think his men are trained in night tactics, but with Gerickman you can't be sure," Weselmann replied.

"When Gerickman left, did you hear any engine sounds?" Wallace asked.

"No."

"Then his main body is in walking distance. How about you and I paying Herr Gerickman a visit tonight?

"Who's in charge while we're sneaking around in the woods? If something happens to one of us," Weselmann asked.

"Sergeant Rickett is as good as they get in our army. If I get killed, he'll hold up my end of the bargain. Will Corporal Vopel do as well?"

"We both have good number two men. Hans will honor any request I make."

"OK, we leave Rickett in charge. How many men do we take with us?"

"The more we take, the more chance we'll be discovered," Weselmann replied.

"Then it's just the two of us."

"That's fine with me."

"Good, how about showing me how the MP40 works?" Wallace asked, pushing open the heavy wooden door of the church.

Inside Stazinski was bandaging up Billings' leg, while Perry and Piontek sat on benches smoking cigarettes, trying to communicate. Due to their wounds, neither was going to be able to fight any offensive action.

"Didn't know you spoke German, Perry"

"I don't. He doesn't speak English either, but he's trying," he said, pointing to Piontek who continued to jabber something unintelligible about the cigarette he was holding.

"How's the shoulder?"

"Hurts like crazy, sir."

"Looks like a million-dollar wound, you'll be home before Thanksgiving. Think about that when it hurts again," replied

Wallace, bringing a smile to Perry's face before the pain of his shoulder made him wince.

Turning to the medic and Billings he asked, "How bad is it, Doc?"

"Clean wound. He'll be all right."

"That means I get to go home, Lieutenant." Billings hopefully asked.

"Sorry, I'll punch your ticket for a week or two in an aid station, but then you'll be back in the line with us."

The young soldier shrugged his shoulders before picking up his M1 and exiting the church. Wallace worried the most about kids like Billings. Being a replacement they didn't seem to last long.

"Anybody else hurt out there?" Stazinski asked.

"You might check Corporal Vopel. He had some kind of arm wound."

The medic exited the church as Weselmann and Wallace walked to a closet where the spare German weapons had been deposited.

Selecting the best-looking MP40 in the lot and several clips, they climbed the stairs to the steeple.

Night had closed on the French countryside, and the forest looked black except for a series of lights about a kilometer to the east.

"That makes a nice beacon for an air attack," Baumann commented.

"Wish we had a radio, we could end this real quick," replied Wallace. "How's your ammo?"

"Two clips left."

"Get one of the German Mausers from the closet downstairs and bring up enough ammo for yourself and your buddy."

"Then you think after the shellacking we gave them, they'll be back?"

"Yeah, you can count on it," Wallace said.

"Then he'll be back for the stuff that's hidden in the church."

"What stuff is that?"

"The stuff that was hidden in the staff car. The valuables and French money."

"How do you know about that?"

"My partner filled me in," he said, tilting his head towards Baake.

"Well, we're not keeping any of it. When this is over, I'm sending it to Division."

"Right, Lieutenant," Baumann said, exiting the steeple to head for the spare weapons.

"I imagine the rest of your men will soon know about the reason Gerickman keeps coming back," Weselmann said.

"That's fine. They should know why I'm risking their lives," Wallace replied, straining to see anything of importance in the lighted part of the woods.

"*Karl, gehen unten weiter und dehnen Ihre Beine aus. Geben Sie dem Amerikaner eine Hand mit der Munition,*" Weselmann ordered.

The German sharpshooter slung his weapon before exiting down the stairwell.

"What did you tell him?"

"Just to stretch his legs and help your man with the ammunition. Still worried we will betray you?"

"No, I feel confident I can trust you. Just curious."

Realizing there was no point staring into the darkness, the two men sat down on the floor of the steeple, getting out their canteens. Weselmann handed his to Wallace after the lieutenant realized his own canteen was empty.

"Thanks."

"Have you given much thought on what do we do after we defeat Gerickman?" Weselmann asked.

"You and your men could surrender. I guarantee your men will receive fair treatment," said the American, handing the canteen back. "You and your men would survive, spending the rest of the war in a comfortable prison camp."

"I can't do that."

"Why, still think your side will win this war?"

"No, I have no doubt you will win this war."

"When did you come to that realization?"

"When the Jabos decimated our panzers without any interference from Goering's Luftwaffe, I still had hope. When your artillery broke up our attacks again and again, hope slowly faded. It was the sight of hundreds of bombers heading for Germany. That kind of power will ultimately spell doom for our side," Weselmann reflected.

"Then give up. It's just a matter of time before Hitler and his gang are finished."

"We don't fight for the Führer anymore. We fight to get our comrades home to their families, not world domination. And my duty is to get back to 3rd Company and help them get back home as well."

"I'm giving you a chance to keep all your men alive to survive this war."

"Why don't you surrender to me?" Weselmann asked, already knowing the answer.

"What? You know I can't do that," Wallace replied.

"That's right. We both have a duty, an oath of loyalty. I can't give up anymore than you could."

"Well, I see your point."

"I do have one request, if I must leave any wounded behind after this; I ask that you see they get that fair treatment you mentioned."

"That I can promise you," Wallace said.

The sound of Baake and Baumann climbing the stairs brought their conversation to an end. Both carried an extra rifle and several bandoliers of ammunition. Baumann also carried a bag of bottles that clattered with each step he took.

"What do we have here, Private?" Wallace asked suspiciously, thinking he had liberated a wine cellar.

"It's the German corporal's idea, sir. Empty wine bottles filled with gasoline, said the Russians used them against their tanks," Baumann said. "Just light the rag stuffed in the bottle and throw it; he said it's a very effective weapon. From this steeple, we may be able to knock out the remaining half-track."

"How effective are they?" Wallace asked.

"In 1942, our company was escorting a squadron of twelve Mark III panzers into a town in Central Russia when attacked by Cossacks on horseback. Heedless of the casualties we inflicted on them, they kept coming. A few slipped through our lines, throwing their Molotov cocktails at several of the panzers, before we could stop them. The bottles smashed against the hulls and turrets, the gasoline exploded penetrating the panzer's interiors, burning the crews alive. To this day I still can hear their screams of agony," an emotional Weselmann reflected. "Use them only as a last resort. Even a Gestapo man deserves a better death than that."

Putting his hand on Weselmann's shoulder, Wallace said, "Come on. Let's get a little sleep before going on that night patrol."

Descending the steps, they saw the young woman entering her private chambers at the opposite side of the church. Still she wore traditional French attire instead of her nun's habit.

Weselmann stopped at the bottom of the steeple stairs. "I want to see if she is all right. Her world has been turned upside down in the last two days. Her faith in God has been sorely tested." Weselmann said.

"She's not wearing her nun's outfit. You know anything about that?"

"Only that she feels all this is her fault, and she is not worthy to be a nun."

"She can't help that there are animals like Gerickman in this world," Wallace replied.

"I know. I tried to explain to her that she, above all, is an innocent victim of our situation. I'm more responsible than she. I started all this when I killed Otto Gerickman."

"If I were in your shoes, I would have killed him myself." Checking his watch under the light of a candle, Wallace continued, "Meet me out front at midnight. Don't be too long. Get some sleep. I want you wide awake for that patrol," he said, walking out into the night air.

Franz waited for five minutes trying to formulate what to say before knocking on the door leading to the nun's quarters. He waited a few minutes but there was no answer. He decided to leave and get some sleep when the door opened and a soft voice said, "Franz, don't go."

She opened the door wide enough for Weselmann to enter her quarters. On a small table, lit by several candles, was her Bible apparently opened to a certain chapter and verse. Two worn chairs near the table led Weselmann to believe that this is where the two nuns carried out their nightly devotions.

"Please sit down, Franz," she said, offering the chair opposite her, but he continued standing.

"How are you feeling?"

Ignoring his question, she asked with tears forming in her eyes, "There was so much shooting. How many more men died because of me?"

"Only Herr Gerickman's men are dying. My men and the Americans are fine."

"I'm glad your men are well, but men are dying because of me."

"That's not true."

"Please, don't say it's your fault because you defended me."

"Herr Gerickman continues to come here, not for revenge but for wealth stolen from the French Jews that was hidden in his brother's car. He is greedy not bound to honor for his brother."

"But all this started because of what happened to his brother and that is my fault," she sobbed.

"How in God's name when he kills Sister Genevieve and does the terrible things to you, is it still your fault?" Weselmann said with a look of astonishment in his eyes.

"I should have never screamed. Had I kept silent, he would still be alive, and his men would not be dead because of his actions."

Weselmann shook his head slowly in unbelief then took his helmet off before sitting down. Forming his hands as though he were praying, he rested his chin on his extended thumbs, trying to think of the right words to tell her.

"Michelle, if I had not killed Otto Gerickman, other women would have suffered the same fate. There was no excuse for his actions. He was an evil man. You are blameless."

"But you killed him, because of me. 'Vengeance is mine, I will repay, saith the Lord'," she said.

"Maybe God's wrath descended on his head in the form of Franz Weselmann. I have felt guilt for the many men I have killed during this war, but I feel no guilt at all for killing Otto Gerickman. He deserved to die," he coldly said.

"Oh Franz, part of me wants to be with you and part of me feels I need to continue as a nun. I don't know what to do?" Michelle said, reaching across the table to take his hand.

Holding her slender hand, he softly said, "I do care about you, but you'll never be happy unless you choose the right path. The answer is in the book in front of you. God will show you the direction you should go. Somewhere in Psalms, it says 'I will instruct thee and teach thee in the way which thou shalt go: I will guide with mine eye'."

"I knew you were special the moment we first met. I haven't felt this way towards another man since my husband was killed."

At a loss for words, he slowly rose from the table looking into her lovely, brown eyes. He too felt a warmth in his heart that he could not dismiss. A warmth that went beyond merely caring for her.

"We'll talk later," he softly said, replacing his helmet and walking to the door.

"I'll pray for you. Please be careful, Franz."

"I will, goodnight, Michelle."

Closing the door behind him, he climbed the stairs to the church sanctuary. Stopping at the altar he knelt down before looking at the image of Jesus on the cross, then whispered, "Please Lord, give her the guidance she needs." He then quickly exited the church to find a quiet place to get some sleep, hoping the path she would choose included him.

Chapter 16

Night mercifully fell over the French landscape hiding, the mangled bodies of the two opposing armies. The incessant assaults had driven Hauptmann Dietz's men back from their original position, but a dusk counterattack restored the line for the night. A relative calm had settled over the area, punctuated only by the faint sounds of artillery in the distance.

A German medic was bandaging a wound that Dietz had received leading the last counterattack. The German captain sat on the edge of his dugout, looking at some of the dead that were so close that even the night could not conceal their violent ends. Two very young soldiers lay together; each one had killed the other with his own trench knife. Each soldier's face had that vacant look of surprise as death overcame him. Dietz recognized the young German as a replacement who had just joined his company before the advance to the front. His dead eyes asking his commander, *why*?

Everything was ready for the night withdrawal when Lieutenant Krueger reported in.

"How is the arm, Herr Hauptmann?

"It will be fine, Klaus," Dietz replied, glad his concentration on the dead youth was broken.

A shriek of pain escaped from his lips as he scolded the medic, "Not so tight, Heinrich."

"Sorry, sir," the medic replied, loosening the wrap.

"Get a few men to move these two boys," he winced, pointing to the dead soldiers at the edge of his dugout.

The medic nodded before exiting to get some help.

Regaining his composure Dietz's asked, "What's all the commotion?"

"Herr Hauptmann, there appears to be a German unit fighting on our left flank, about a kilometer from our lines."

"Hauptmann Hauser's men?"

"We're not sure, could be them."

"According to our latest intelligence, there shouldn't be any American units coming from that direction."

"Partisans?"

"Well, if it is partisans, they won't have heavy weapons. Is Ritter's platoon ready to pull back?"

"Yes, sir."

A very young, wounded panzer grenadier, his arm in a sleeve, was walking past when he was stopped by Dietz.

"Hubbell, you're from Unterfeldwebel Ritter's platoon, tell him I want to see him now."

"I can't do that, sir," he sorrowfully responded.

"Why not?"

"He was killed in the last assault, Herr Hauptmann."

Looking away into his dugout, he let out a sigh, thinking Ritter was a good soldier. Too many good soldiers have died in this war. How much longer before the bullet comes that keeps him from ever seeing his wife and children again. Returning back to the young man, he asked, "How was he killed?"

"Unterfeldwebel Ritter and four men charged an American machine gun position. The other four went to ground when the Americans fired, but he still advanced and was struck several times before throwing a stick grenade that destroyed the American gun."

Slowly reaching into his jacket pocket, he retrieved the company roster making a few notes by Ritter's name before marking the man as deceased. Glancing through the remaining names of Ritter's he asked, "Who is next in rank?"

"I'm not sure who it is. There are so few of us left." The young soldier's tears slowly traveled down his face.

"Go back and find out who it is and send him to me," he said, his heart aching for the young man standing before him.

"Jahowl, Herr Hauptmann," he responded, heading in a southward direction towards his unit.

Waiting until the young man disappeared into the darkness, Dietz asked, "What are our casualties?"

"Sixty-seven available, half of them are wounded, but can still fight."

"How many dead?"

"Since we built the roadblock, twenty-four."

"Ammunition?"

"There is no more ammunition for the mortars or the MG42s. One panzersheck round left. Less than forty percent of small arm munitions are left as well."

"How's the general morale, Klaus?"

His aide enthusiastically responded, "We have stopped them again and again, Herr Hauptmann. The men's morale is greatly improved. We are winning."

"Well, I'm sure that the Führer will be greatly impressed by our victory in spite of all our recent defeats," Dietz sarcastically replied.

"But, Herr Hauptmann, if we can hold them here, maybe reinforcements will be sent for a counterattack."

"Let's be realistic. Look at the men we receive as replacements; rather, look at the boys we receive. We are running out of people to fight with. How are we going to win the war with boys? I need experienced men."

"But, the Führer promised us victory. We have new, super weapons coming to defeat the Allies. Don't spread defeatist rumors, Herr Hauptmann," Krueger said, whose tone and demeanor troubled Dietz.

"It is not defeatist to want the weapons and manpower that I need to destroy Germany's enemies," he sternly told his aide. "The bravest man in the world is no match for a pride of lions without his weapons."

"I'm sorry, Herr Hauptmann. I know you are an excellent officer. I'm just discouraged that we keep retreating."

"Klaus, you too can become a good officer. A good officer knows what his men can accomplish," Dietz replied, seeing a slightly overweight soldier approaching.

The weary looking soldier came to attention in front of Dietz. "Herr Hauptmann, you wanted to see me."

"You are taking over Ritter's platoon?"

"Yes, sir. All the other non-coms above my rank are dead or wounded."

"How many men do you have left?"

"Not counting the wounded, I have fourteen men, Herr Hauptmann."

"I don't recognize you. When did you join our company?"

"Just before the last attack I wandered into Unterfeldwebel Ritter's position after losing contact with my own unit. He needed an experienced squad leader, and I needed a unit to adopt."

"What is your name and unit?"

"Unteroffizier Heinrich Weber, 3rd Company, sir."

"Kurt Hauser's company, where are they?" he asked the excitement apparent in his voice.

"I don't know, Herr Hauptmann, I was part of the rearguard and was separated from them when the American tanks broke through our lines. I have been wandering through these woods for days, looking for other German troops."

Dietz pulled out his map and handed it to Weber. "Show me where the rearguard was located."

Using a small flashlight, he scanned the map for several minutes, before finding a familiar landmark.

"Here, Herr Hauptmann."

"That's forty kilometers southwest of our present position. Which direction did your company head?"

"Hauptmann Hauser figured the Americans would already be at the crossroads, so he headed northeast through the woods."

Dietz stood up looking into the darkness, placing his hands on his belt. It made Weber a little nervous the way he stood looking into the shadows evidently contemplating some action.

"I have a mission for you, Weber. Take ten men and scout out the firing on our left flank. It might be your 3rd Company. Set your watch to 9:13 PM, we will stay here until 2:00 AM, and if you are not back with news of 3rd Company we are pulling out."

"Yes, sir," he said, leaving to collect his men.

"Then are we staying past two o'clock if Hauser's men are near by, Herr Hauptmann?" asked his aide.

"Yes, Klaus. If Hauser is out there, God help me, I'm risking our lives to save them. But if all goes according to plan, our combined companies will be able to fight back to our lines."

"But Herr Hauptmann, where are our lines?"

"Unfortunately, the way our army is withdrawing, it could be across the Rhine River."

The young aide slumped against the dugout wall wondering if he or any of 2nd Company would rejoin the Regiment. The minutes dragged on as Dietz and Krueger waited for news of Kurt Hauser's missing company. The Americans seemed content to wait until morning before launching any attacks as the frontline outposts reported in: all was quiet. Krueger kept checking his watch disappointed that the time moved so slowly.

"Relax, Klaus. Try and get some sleep."

"I can't sleep, worrying if Hauptmann Hauser will show up."

Dietz's comments were quickly followed by the sound of gunfire coming from the left flank, which broke the monotony of the night. Grabbing their helmets and weapons, they moved as quickly as the night would allow, avoiding loose equipment and shell holes until they reached the last outpost on the left flank. Several panzer grenadiers spun around ready to fire before recognizing the two officers who joined them in the dry creek bed.

"Any sign of Weber's patrol?"

"No, Herr Hauptmann," a grimy looking private replied.

"How long has he been gone?"

"About an hour and a half."

"Appears quiet as a graveyard. How long since you heard anything?"

"After the firing stopped five minutes ago, nothing, Herr Hauptmann."

The ground directly in front of the position was littered with helmets, weapons, discarded equipment and bodies. The effect of the artillery barrages was in evidence as well as violently ripped tree limbs were lying everywhere.

Dietz peered into the shadows trying hard to see any movement in the darkened woods when a tree branch snapped off to the right. All weapons and eyes were trained on the darkness in the direction of the sound.

"Don't fire unless you can tell it's the enemy. Remember our men are out there," Dietz cautioned, balancing the barrel of his MP40 on the lip of the creek bank.

The next moments seemed an eternity as the sounds of men moving became more apparent to the men in the creek bed. Dietz could imagine the fingers on the triggers of the weapons around him slowly tightening, waiting for the sign, any sign that the men stirring in the woods were American. A familiar shape loomed out of the darkness followed by another, then another, as the men relaxed.

"Herr Hauptmann, there are more than ten men. Weber has found 3rd Company!" Krueger blurted, genuine joy in his voice.

As the men of the two companies greeted each other, a tall, handsome officer looked at the soldiers around Dietz. "Where is your commander?"

"Here, Oberleutnant."

The young officer snapped to attention. "Sorry, Herr Hauptmann. I didn't recognize you. Oberleutnant Helmut Brock, 3rd Company."

"Forget the apology. Where is Hauptmann Hauser?" Dietz replied, looking down at his bloody, dirty uniform.

"Hauptmann Hauser and the rest of our company are about two hours behind us, he said, pointing to the southwest. "My platoon and all the wounded were sent ahead."

"We heard shooting. Who were you fighting?"

"A group of partisans attacked us but were beaten off when they realized that we were not a small patrol."

"Do you have any extra ammunition?"

"Yes, sir. We found an abandoned supply truck, shot up in a ditch, but most of its cargo intact. Hauptmann Hauser had us take as much as we could carry."

"Anti-tank weapons?"

"We have five panzerfausts."

"Good, we have something beside our bare hands to destroy their tanks."

"Herr Hauptmann, do we stay?" Krueger asked.

"Yes, Klaus we will wait for rest of Hauptmann Hauser's men. Schmidt's platoon has the most ground to cover. Brock, will you take your men and reinforce the center of our line. Lieutenant Krueger will show where I want your men emplaced."

"Yes, sir," replied Brock, signaling his men to follow Krueger.

Weber's men were the last troops in the parade. He stopped briefly, saluting Dietz.

"Well done, Weber. You will retain command of this platoon until I can find someone else, unless you would like to transfer to my company."

"Thank you, sir, but I would like to return to my own company whenever Herr Hauptmann can find a replacement for me."

"Very well, I understand. Your comrades are in 3rd Company. Carry on, Weber."

Looking at his watch and seeing it was 1:37 AM, Dietz calculated that Hauser would arrive shortly before dawn. They could hold another day, as Brock's platoon would replace the majority of his losses, and he now had some weapons to stop enemy tanks. Walking to his dugout, he noticed the look of confidence had returned to his men's faces as he passed them. The gloom of waiting for news of missing comrades was replaced by the elation of knowing that soon they would be reunited. Stepping down into his dugout, he thought now I can relax. He was right. In minutes, he was sound asleep.

Chapter 17

Five minutes before midnight Weselmann arrived at the front of the church finding Wallace rubbing a black compound on his face. The American tossed the can to the German sergeant who darkened his own face. Replacing their helmets with their comfortable fatigue caps, they also left their machine pistols in favor of sidearm pistols to travel as light and quiet as possible. Wallace handed Weselmann a couple of American grenades before stuffing two more in his own tunic.

"Are you sure about this, Lieutenant?" Rickett asked.

"Yes, I want to know what Gerickman's up to. If everything is quiet, then he won't be back until morning. But if he is planning a night attack, we'll know it and may even get close enough to hear his plans."

"I still think you're both nuts to go on this night patrol."

"May I second that motion? What if Herr Gerickman attacks before you two can get back here?" Vopel asked anxiously.

"Hans, you sound like a mother hen, don't worry. We'll be fine. You know this isn't my first night patrol," Weselmann said, grinning at his friend.

"Keep alert. Gerickman might pull something before morning, but I doubt it," Wallace ordered the two men.

"The sentries know you're going out, password is cabbage and countersign is patch," Rickett said.

Without another word the two men disappeared into the darkness of the woods, as Vopel and Rickett shook their heads in silent opposition to their mission.

The temperature had dropped rapidly after the sun had set. At first it was a relief but now damp cold air was not only uncomfortable but with each breath a telltale mist was left in the air. As they moved slowly through the thick woods, Wallace stopped suddenly when he smelled the odor of cigarette smoke. Weselmann, after scanning the woods, tapped the American lieutenant on the shoulder pointing twenty yards to their left where the faint glow of a cigarette stood out in the darkness. Gerickman had set a sentry post about a hundred yards from the village.

Moving quietly to the right, they discovered a second outpost thirty yards from the first one, given away by the nervous chatter of its occupants. Using the ground fog as cover, they began to crawl through Gerickman's first line of defense when a twig-snapping sound made the talkative Gestapo men suspicious. Hugging the ground they waited as the beam of a flashlight moved backward and forward in their direction. Satisfied that an animal had made the noise, the chatter started up again.

For the next fifty yards, they crawled at a snail's pace, halting every five or six yards as their ears strained for any human sounds, until they were sure they were well past the Gestapo sentry posts. They resumed their earlier pace for fifteen minutes before seeing the glow of a fire about a kilometer from the village. Inching closer towards the light, they stopped at the edge of a small clearing, just off the dirt road.

Looking carefully into the darkness they could make out the silhouettes of Gerickman's vehicles tucked as close as possible to the tree line. The small fire burned near the center of the camp with no one attending to it.

"Strange, I don't see any sentries," Wallace whispered.

"Can't believe that Herr Gerickman would take the precaution of the advanced outposts and not set sentries for the night," Weselmann whispered back.

"I'm going closer for a better look. Wait here."

Wallace darted from the cover of the woods, running to the rear of the nearest truck, while Weselmann covered him from the woods. Motioning Weselmann to join him, he heard the sounds of sleeping men inside the vehicle. The usually nimble sergeant stumbled on a tree root and bumped into the side of the truck.

Wallace, pulling his pistol from its holster, gave the German an anxious look as an occupant of the truck stirred inside. Weselmann slowly shook his head as he pulled a knife from his boot. He slipped past Wallace, moving as close as possible to the back of the truck without leaving the protection of the shadows. A lone SS man jumped down from the truck, bareheaded and unarmed. He stood stretching his stiff muscles and then walked to the tree line to relieve himself. After accomplishing his task, he returned to his truck unaware how close he had come to Weselmann's deadly blade.

Returning the knife to its previous location, Weselmann and Wallace both let out a muted sigh of relief, as the Gestapo man apparently resumed sleeping.

Moving to a position away from the vehicles, Wallace whispered, "That was too close. That guy will never know how close he came to being worm food."

"I'm glad we didn't have to kill him. I dislike killing in close quarters," Weselmann whispered in reply.

"That's because you're not a killer. You do it because, like me, it's your job, not because you enjoy it. I pity the ones in both of our armies who kill and get pleasure out of it."

"There they are," Weselmann said, nodding to the far end of the clearing. The missing sentries, caught in the light of the fire, appeared to be milling around the back of a command car.

"That's could be Otto Gerickman's car. I wonder why the sentries are just guarding his vehicle."

Weselmann observed the actions of the Gestapo men. "Look at them, they're not guarding his car, they're searching it."

"If we follow the tree line to the left, we could hear what they're saying. There's plenty of cover and they shouldn't be able to spot us," Wallace said.

"But is it worth the risk?"

"Curiosity. I want to know what's going on with these boys, besides we could learn some information that'll give our men a better edge when Gerickman attacks."

"Don't you Americans have a saying, 'curiosity killed the cat'," Weselmann asked.

Grinning at his companion, Wallace started moving slowly to the desired area of the forest, followed by Weselmann. Halting every few feet, they peered towards the sentries who continued to be more interested in the staff car than the surrounding woods. The two men slid silently to the ground where the voices of the sentries could be heard, not every word but enough to get the gist of the conservation.

Five Gestapo men were examining the contents of the late Otto Gerickman's trunk and from their reactions they didn't find anything of value.

A tall, rugged-looking SS corporal said, "Well whatever keeps us going back to that lousy village isn't here. I wager our beloved Otto Gerickman's staff car had something of value to our commander. Weselmann's men must have it."

"After our losses today, I hope Herr Gerickman's plan works. Those traitors and their American friends cut our men to ribbons. Another attack like that one and all of us can stop worrying about anything," a SS man, with a MP40 slung across his back, replied.

A fairly young looking Gestapo man said nervously, "Shouldn't we be a little more quiet. We'll wake the officers up."

"Are you blind as well as stupid? All the officers went back to the warm beds of the next village hours ago. Herr Gerickman won't be back until morning. He's ordered Goetz's squad to get one of the Weselmann's men alive for interrogation before our next attack," the tall SS corporal scoffed.

"And the mood he was in when he returned from talking with the Americans, I wouldn't want to be any captive of his right now," a SS man responded, casually leaning against the half-track.

"Which of our previous captives would you have been, Rolf?"

"Your right, they all get our special treatment," he replied with a laugh.

"There's nothing else for us here. You four get back to your sentry posts. Goetz's men will be back soon. I'm going to get some sleep," the corporal said, heading for the half-track.

A startled Weselmann gave Wallace an anxious look. "We need to get back fast."

"What did he say?" Wallace asked.

"No time to explain now. We need to get back," Weselmann replied, melting into the darkness. Wallace quickly followed the suddenly upset German sergeant.

There was no sign of concern of discovery from Weselmann as he veered north towards the road. Wallace wondered what the Gestapo man said that caused this German to abandon all caution. Only after reaching the road did Weselmann slow his pace.

"Do you want to tell me what spooked you back there?" Wallace whispered angrily, grabbing the sleeve of Weselmann's tunic."

"Gerickman sent men to our village to capture one of us. If successful, they would bring any captive back down the road instead of traveling through the woods."

Understanding his companion's concern for his men, he released his grip. "What else did you learn?"

"Herr Gerickman and his officers are spending the night in the next village and he wasn't planning an attack until he interrogated one of us. I'm sorry, but I have seen what Gestapo methods can do to human beings. I will not allow that to happen to any of my men or yours if I can help it."

"Next time, just let me know what you're doing."

"I won't —," Weselmann suddenly stopped speaking as he peered into the darkness of the road. The faint sounds of boots on the dirt road were becoming more distinct with each second.

Out of the darkness, the shapes of four men emerged, three were armed and helmeted, and the fourth was obviously bareheaded and bound. Their faces were indistinguishable, but Weselmann recognized the build and mannerisms of the fourth man as Private Fritz Stempel. One Gestapo man, with an MP40, led the graying veteran who was flanked by a SS man on either side.

Wallace pulled his combat knife, indicating to Weselmann, who drew his knife as well, with hand signals to let the leader pass and which guard to take out. The adrenaline started to flow as the two men crouched, ready to spring upon Stempel's captors. Wallace picked up a small rock. Just before the leader went past their location, he arched the rock over the heads of the guards landing in the woods on the other side of the road. Distracted momentarily, the leader paused his men before taking a couple steps towards the sound, his MP40 at the ready.

Simultaneously, the two hidden men closed on the guards around Stempel. Wallace's left hand reached up grabbing the front of the nearest German's helmet, wrenching it back hard. The helmet's strap cut off any cry as the blade in his right hand went deep into the hard muscle of SS man's back. The brief struggle was over in seconds as the Gestapo man collapsed against Wallace who silently lowered him to the ground. Looking to his partner, he saw Weselmann was already moving towards the leader past the lifeless figure of the second guard. The leader, due to a possible sixth sense, spun around with his machine pistol, firing a burst that barely missed Weselmann who fell to the ground reaching for his Luger. The Gestapo man didn't get a second chance as several slugs from Wallace's .45 caliber pistol smashed into his sternum, knocking him into the woods.

From the woods on their left came a cry, "*Was ist los, Gunther?*"

Wallace untied Stempel's hands and removed the gag from his mouth. "Let's get the hell out of here!"

A MG42 opened up from the woods firing blindly at the spot where Wallace stood only moments before. Following the road, they stayed in the overgrowth at the tree line, but kept up a swift pace in case any Germans from the camp were in pursuit. Reaching the line of outposts, they threw grenades in the general direction of the Gestapo dugouts before covering the remaining distance to Nueviant.

Reaching the village, a challenge came, "Cabbage."

"Patch," Wallace replied unenthusiastically.

Vopel and Rickett, alerted by the firefight, ran up to the three exhausted men who literally stumbled and fell into the sentry post.

"Well, was it worth the risk?" Rickett asked.

Looking at a grateful World War I veteran, Wallace and Weselmann grinned before saying almost in unison, "Yes, it was."

Chapter 18

An hour before dawn, Gerickman in his black BMW staff car, accompanied by his officers, pulled up to where he left his men. He had not slept well, concerned with the possibility he may never know the location of the missing valuables. He hoped that Goetz's patrol would bring a prisoner that knew the location, or he would have to settle for half the treasure. It wasn't worth getting killed for what might not even be in Nueviant anymore. No, he thought, I will have those valuables, they are mine. As his driver opened his door, he had a pleasant thought. Goetz might have captured Weselmann or Vopel.

Sitting in his car, he waited as his officers disembarked to organize their individual units alongside their perspective vehicles. As he stared in the general direction of Nueviant, he reflected on how he came to this point. He thought of Weselmann, the Wehrmacht sergeant who was the cause of all his trouble. He will pay for his insolence. Who was he to pass judgment on Otto, especially for so called crimes against French peasants? What are their lives compared to that of a Gestapo officer. They are nothing. Otto could have killed a hundred, and Weselmann still would not have the right to judge him. Yes, he and all his men, they will pay. If I don't kill him myself, I guarantee, when I get to Strasbourg, I'll see to it somebody does it for me.

Stepping out of his car, he walked towards several officers talking to their men. In the pre-dawn light he stumbled over what appeared to a blanket covered piece of equipment, his wire rim glasses falling from his face.

"Goetz! Who left this equipment lying around." he exclaimed, annoyed with the sergeant he left in charge.

After receiving no answer, he yelled, "Goetz, where are you?"

A SS corporal slowly approached Gerickman. "Herr Strumbannführer."

"Yes, what is it?"

"It is about Unterscharführer Goetz."

"Where is he?" he shrieked, all his patience gone.

The Gestapo man did not say a word; he merely bent down, flipping the blanket off the bundle, revealing the corpse of the late Sergeant Goetz, his chest a mangled mess of bone and dried blood.

"Who did this?" Gerickman asked without emotion, bending down to pickup his glasses.

"We're not sure. They were escorting one of the panzer grenadiers, when attacked on the road. Could have been partisans. They will attack small groups at night," the corporal replied, choosing his words carefully, remembering the fate of Private Meier.

Gerickman lifted the blankets revealing the bodies of two more Gestapo men, wincing in revulsion at the sight of a slit throat. Finding only his own men, he asked, "Where is the prisoner's body?"

"We only found Goetz's men. There was no sign of the captive," hesitating for a moment he continued, "The partisans must have taken him."

"Partisans? What would the partisans want with a Wehrmacht soldier, you idiot? It was that scum of a sergeant, Weselmann again!" Gerickman's voice rising with each word until the entire camp took notice.

The officers and men slowly gathered to their commander as he continued ranting against the SS corporal.

"I'm surrounded by fools! All I ask is that you bring seven men to justice, and what do I get? Nothing but failure. You are not worthy to be Gestapo men. You are all failing the Führer and me. We are going back to the village and we're going to kill anyone who stands in our way."

As he spoke, the diesel engine of the lone half-track gunned to life, edging towards the unhappy commander.

"I gave no orders to move out. What is going on?"

Parting the sea of men, the half-track moved to within ten feet of Gerickman before stopping. From within the vehicle, a sinister sounding voice asked, "Herr Strumbannführer needs to explain why he continues to attack the village and risk our lives?"

Recognizing the voice, he angrily replied, "I do not need to explain my actions to you, Mueller. You will follow orders or be court-martialed."

Slinging open the door to the half-track, Mueller stepped out, his MP40 ready for use. Gerickman noticed one of the corporal's crew had manned the half-track's MG42, with the barrel pointed directly at his chest. The looks in the eyes of his men told him many of them wanted an answer to Mueller's question. More would side with his corporal, if he tried to arrest or kill him.

"Is this a mutiny then?" Gerickman said calmly, folding his hands behind his back, trying to defuse the situation.

"No, Herr Gerickman, we are all loyal Nazis, but I do not wish to throw my life away. For two days this action, against the forces in Nueviant, has caused the death of over fifty men. What is so important that we keep dying in that village?" Mueller replied.

"You know why we keep going back to that village; those Wehrmacht pigs killed my brother. I will see that they pay for their crime," he said, trying to convince his men it was his only motive. "All I want is revenge for Otto's murder."

"Sir, I have always had respect for you, but your brother was more trouble than he was worth. Everyone knew sooner or later a petticoat would be the cause of his death."

Thinking that he might be able to turn the tables on his corporal he agreed with him. "Yes, I know, Mueller. But that does not excuse Weselmann killing him." Gerickman just needed to bide some time. No one had ever survived angering the SS major and as far as he was concerned, no one would. In his own mind, Mueller and his friends were dead men.

"Well if that is the only reason, you wouldn't object to us looking in the trunk of your car, sir," a very sly corporal replied, taking a step closer.

"I do object. Who do you think you are, Mueller? Enough of this foolishness. You have two men, and I have over eighty." Turning to a young SS lieutenant, he ordered, "Ludwig, arrest this man and his co-conspirators."

The young officer drew his pistol, taking a step towards the corporal, but half a dozen men blocked his path. Seeing the hopelessness of the situation, he returned his weapon to its holster. "I think the best solution to our problem is to let Mueller look in your trunk, Herr Strumbannführer."

Looking at the faces of his men, Gerickman realized that either he had to tell them the truth or only count on a few to remain loyal. He might survive this confrontation but the odds were not good. Too many had died in the fruitless attempts to recover the missing treasure and before his remaining men would enter the village again, he needed to give them a better reason than his brother's murder.

"Very well, I am carrying the valuables of the Jewish detainees from Nancy; or rather I have half of the valuables. Weselmann and his traitors stole the articles in the trunk of Hauptsturmführer Gerickman's staff car. He killed Otto and the others for greed and not a trifle with a French peasant. These possessions and what remain in Nueviant belong to the Führer whom you all swore an oath to remain loyal to the death. The gold and the jewels belong to the Führer. I can't stomach the idea of Weselmann and his men growing old in luxury with Germany's rightful wealth."

Gerickman could tell he was swaying some of his doubters as their eyes fell to the ground in shame. To a SS man, the name of the Führer had a mesmerizing effect. To retrieve the valuables for Adolf Hitler was worth the risk of death.

"Then, Herr Strumbannführer was merely trying to retrieve the stolen goods of the Führer," Mueller replied in an apologetic tone.

"Yes, Mueller, I was just doing my duty as a loyal Nazi," said Gerickman, convinced that even the despised corporal before him had taken the bait.

"I'm sorry, sir, that I doubted you," said Mueller, giving a sharp salute as he turned to leave, but he stopped and slowly returned his gaze back to Gerickman. "There is one small item that doesn't make sense, sir."

"What is it, Mueller?" Gerickman replied, his patience fading.

Mueller stood with his hand behind his back like a small child ready to surprise his mother on her birthday, but the surprise was not pleasant as his hand emerged with a familiar ledger from Otto's staff car. Gerickman's jaw slightly dropped as he realized all he had just told them could be proven a lie in moments.

"Could you explain this notebook, Herr Strumbannführer?"

"It is a ledger, containing the details of the Führer's possessions. There is some significance to this?" Gerickman nervously replied, trying to regroup his thoughts.

"Yes, sir, there is. Would you explain why this ledger, taken from your brother's staff car only a couple of hours ago, shows anything of value, taken from the Jews, has already been sent to Berlin? Has this ledger been doctored to hide the true amounts of the valuables? Herr Gerickman, have you been hoarding from the Führer?"

The majority of the men, who had been dispersing to their vehicles, gathered again for an explanation. Their faces no longer reflected shame but rather betrayal, asking with their eyes, "How could our commander, a loyal Nazi, betray the Führer?"

"Believe what you wish about the ledger. The fact remains the rightful owner of the valuables is our Führer. If you think I stole from the Führer, then I will turn myself in to the proper authorities, but only after we settle with the traitors in Nueviant. Weselmann and the rest have what belongs to Germany. Can you live with the knowledge of those traitors enjoying that which does not belong to them," pleaded Gerickman, knowing his life was on the line. He felt uncomfortable asking his men to believe him. They should obey, no matter what the circumstances. He was after all their superior officer.

"Then Herr Strumbannführer will turn over all the valuables to the headquarters in Strasbourg?" Bauer asked.

"Yes, Bauer. That is exactly what I intended to do. In the confusion of our departure, inaccurate entries were written in the ledger," Gerickman replied in a firm voice, his eyes never leaving the rebellious Mueller standing before him.

Mueller rolled his eyes in total unbelief to the gullible SS lieutenant's question, realizing Gerickman was convincing, at least the officers, of his innocence of stealing from the Führer. One by one the men returned to their duties, at least for now believing their commander. Gerickman's apparent victory forced Mueller to sling his MP40, which brought a cruel smile to Gerickman's face. He saluted his commander half heartily before entering the armored cab of his vehicle. He told his driver, "Backup, Guenther. Herr Gerickman wins this round, but it is a long way to Strasbourg."

"I don't like the way he's looking at us," Guenther replied.

"Don't worry. He needs the firepower of this vehicle. And no one handles it better than we do. After Nueviant, then you can worry. I still think he plans to steal the valuables."

"He can't do that now. Too many of us know about the treasure," Private Goehl added, leaving the MG42 gun mount.

Mueller removed his helmet, letting it clatter on the floor of the half-track. He leaned back, following Gerickman with his eyes as he said, "If Herr Gerickman has his way there won't be enough of us left alive to stop him. Yes, we'll have to be careful."

Almost as if Gerickman heard the comment, he turned and stared directly at his corporal. The cruel smile was now an evil grin, which chilled the blood of the usually tough Mueller.

Chapter 19

As Gerickman and his officers made their plans for the final assault, the sun slowly unveiled the village of Nueviant. The dew dripped off the leaves and flowers at the start of the new day as the smoking wreckage of the half-track marked the scene of an otherwise peaceful town. The Gestapo bodies had been dumped down a ravine to the south and any breeze from that direction brought the ungodly stench of death with it. The smell from Vopel's pipe was a blessing as it helped to damper the unpleasant odor.

Vopel, Rickett, Goldstein, and Rotter manned a makeshift position watching the road leading to Gerickman's camp. The rest of their men, in shifts of three and four, grabbed as much sleep as possible. All concerned knew this was sure to be the last day of the truce; the main question was how many would survive this day to rejoin their respective units.

From one of the small houses emerged Wallace and Weselmann with the final plan for defending the village. Both knew that the next and possible last attack would be in full force and could come from different directions. Gerickman had seen the folly of sending small groups in piecemeal attacks. This time he would hit and hit hard.

"Any sign of Gerickman, Sergeant?" Wallace yawned.

"Nope, maybe he gave up and moved on, Lieutenant," Rickett replied, hoping it was true.

"Yes, any rational commander would see the folly of another attack, but this man is fanatical. He would sacrifice everyone to retrieve the Jewish belongings. He'll be back," Weselmann said, slumping down alongside Vopel. Shaking his head at Vopel, he continued, "I have a new respect for you Americans, sharing a dugout with the unusual aroma of Hans' pipe."

"I did it only in self-defense, Franz," Vopel replied, tilting his head towards a half-smoked cigar in Rickett's mouth.

"How do you think I feel, Lieutenant? I'm caught in their crossfire," Goldstein said.

"I can remedy that," replied Wallace, reaching down into an open case at his feet. He produced four grenades, handing them to Goldstein. "Reinforce the machine gun crew on the hilltop. If you have to fall back, head for that old foundation at the west end of the village."

"Right, Lieutenant," the young soldier replied, springing out of the position. He paused briefly to toss a casual salute to the men behind, saying with his boyish smile, "Good luck, fellas. See you when we finish with this SS kraut."

Watching Goldstein disappear behind the church, Wallace whispered softly, "I sure hope so, kid."

Looking at Rickett he commented, "I thought you were out of cigars."

"You can thank a SS corporal, who happened to have a couple in his pocket."

"OK. We have already bloodied his nose several times, attacking right up the road, so he should try something different. Any ideas?" asked Wallace.

"He still may use the road. I'd wager the half-track and twenty men will be held in reserve, while he splits the rest of his men into flanking attacks," Rickett theorized.

"What about you, Sergeant Weselmann? If you were Gerickman how would you attack us?"

"I agree with Sergeant Rickett. Draw attention to the flanks to draw you out of your positions, then hit you in platoon strength up the road with the half-track giving covering fire," replied Weselmann.

Turning to Vopel, Wallace received a nod of approval agreeing with the two sergeants.

"But that is how we would attack; the four of us care about the health of our men. Success to us is as few of our men killed or wounded as possible in securing our mission. Gerickman's only concern is recovering what is hidden in the church. If it costs all his men, he would sleep like a baby tonight without regret, as long as he recovers his three chests," Weselmann said.

"Then how do you think he'll attack?"

"He'll do the opposite, keep throwing men and equipment up the road, while sneaking around with a small group to flank us. We'll be too busy with the Gestapo in front of us to watch our flanks."

"After meeting the gentleman, I'm afraid you're right," Wallace replied, scanning the village for the best way to defend such an attack.

The quiet of the early morning was ripped with the crump of heavy artillery plastering the French countryside in the general direction of the German roadblock. Wallace and his companions wondered how long Hauptmann Dietz could hold, while deep inside each man had the desire to finish their private war.

"Those are long toms. If they're on target, that roadblock won't last long," Rickett said.

"Long toms?" Vopel inquired, puffing on his pipe.

"155 MM howitzers," Wallace commented. "Sergeant Rickett is right. Our truce might be over before Gerickman attacks."

"Before we decide to start shooting at one another, do you have a plan just in case Herr Gerickman shows up first?" Vopel asked.

"Right, Gerickman may solve our problem for us. Corporal Vopel, take three of your men and hold the two houses, directly across from the church, on the north side of the village. Sergeant Rickett, pick two men and occupy the foundation and hold there in case Gerickman tries to flank us. Who is on the hilltop?"

"Goldstein, Jenkins, Lepper, Higgins, and Glassman"

"Take Glassman and Higgins for your group. You have two missions, keep our flanks clean and cover the front of the church. We'll barricade the front doors and you keep any intruders from getting in. Any questions?"

"What if they overrun my position?" Vopel asked.

"Fall back to the old foundation and hold with Sergeant Rickett's group."

Turning to Rickett, Vopel smiled. "Remember, we are on your side, at least for today."

"We'll try to hold our fire. Wouldn't want to mess up that pretty panzer grenadier uniform," Rickett replied with a grin.

"What is the signal to start the show, Lieutenant?" Rickett asked.

"We'll open up from the church. Any other questions?" He paused for a moment but there were no other inquiries. "OK, move out. We don't know how much time we have left before Herr Gerickman starts the party," said Wallace.

A tired looking gray-haired panzer grenadier trotted to Weselmann. "Corporal Vopel said to report to you."

"That leaves five of us to hold the church," replied Weselmann.

"With Vopel's group in the houses, Bunzel and Baumann in the steeple, covering fire from the hilltop and the three of us firing from the church windows, we should set up a crossfire that even experienced troops would break and run."

"Of course, that depends on Herr Gerickman attacking up the road in force," Weselmann said.

"Let's pray and believe that God leads him down that road," Wallace replied. "We do have a nun on our side."

The trio entered the church, picking the best spots for the ground floor defense. Wallace motioned Stempel to cover the window closest to the oaken doors. Weselmann felt badly about breaking out firing ports in the beautiful stain glass. But figured God would understand, they were fighting a godless enemy.

"Stazinski, move the wounded to the church basement with Sister Monique. Any Gestapo man that breaks through can be picked off on the staircase."

The young medic helped Piontek to his feet, supporting the panzer grenadier's wounded leg. Perry followed them, holding his hand over his wounded shoulder. Both men winced in pain with each step.

"What if they throw grenades into the basement?" Weselmann questioned, clearly apprehensive about the wounded and the woman he cared for.

"We'll set up crates and anything else to shelter them from any potato mashers the SS might toss down the stairs. And we'll make sure they have plenty of automatic weapons and ammo."

"If the Gestapo does get into the basement, you and I will probably be dead," Weselmann sighed.

"Yeah, I know," Wallace grimly replied.

A soft voice pierced the darkness of the basement stairwell, interrupting their conversation. "Franz, can I talk with you?"

"Excuse me, Lieutenant."

"Go ahead, but make it quick. I'll check with Bunzel and Baumann in the steeple. Gerickman could hit us anytime," said Wallace, wondering if he ever would know how the relationship between the German sergeant and the novice would end.

Weselmann waited until Wallace disappeared up the steeple steps before walking to the young woman, unsure what to say to her. He sought to tell her many things, but now he only wanted to be sure she was safe. If they didn't beat back Gerickman, her fate could be too cruel to contemplate.

She took his hand, leading him to a candlelight corner of the church basement far enough away from Stazinski and the wounded that their conversation could be private. In the light of the candles, for a few moments, he stood admiring her beauty, before their lips met in a tender embrace.

"Oh, Franz please take me with you when leave," she softly pleaded.

"No, Michelle I can't do that. You would be in great danger; you will be safer here until this war is over. The Americans will soon occupy Nueviant, and they are good people. I would take you if I knew you would be safe, but the artillery and fighter-bombers of the Americans do not distinguish between soldiers and civilians in a convoy of troops."

"Will you come back when the war is over?" she asked, tears forming in her eyes.

"Only my death would keep me from returning to you," he softly replied, brushing her tears aside.

"Then, I will wait for you here, praying the Lord will keep you and your men safe."

"I have to go. We have to end this today so that we can be together at the end of this war."

Without a word from either, he took her in his arms, kissing her again before jogging up the stairs to the church sanctuary. Pausing at the altar, he knelt down removing his helmet as he prayed, "Oh Lord, grant us the victory today. Keep my men, the Americans, and Michelle safe from harm. Grant us the courage and strength to defeat the Gestapo. Amen."

Rising to his feet, he thought of many more things he could say to her, but unless Gerickman was stopped there was no point in saying them. He had acquired a new enthusiasm to survive, the need to return to a woman who cared for him.

Placing his helmet back on his head, he proceeded to climb the steeple stairs to join Wallace, who was scanning the forest with his binoculars. Bunzel and Baumann huddled in the corner catching a few minutes sleep while the lieutenant kept watch.

"See anything?"

"No, all seems quiet. Vopel and Rickett are in position. All we need is Herr Gerickman to oblige us with his presence," said Wallace, moving away from the window in case a sniper had a view of his position.

"How's the lady holding up?"

"She'll be fine, provided we win today," Weselmann replied, thinking the term lady had a nice ring to it.

"We'll win. It is just a matter of how many of us survive."

"Survival. In the midst of all this death, that's all I want for my men, and myself," the German sergeant replied, slumping against an unoccupied wall.

Wallace continued to watch the forest, hunting for any signs of movement. "That is all any soldier wants the ability to go home after the war is over."

"What will you do, when this war is over?"

"I imagine I'll return to teaching; that's what I did before the war."

"What did you teach?"

"Mathematics and I coached football."

"Strange, I taught French and English at Augsburg. I too wish to return to my students. I wonder what the odds are of two teachers, who are enemies, fighting a common foe." Weselmann pondered.

"Probably one in a million. How come they didn't make you an officer?" Wallace asked, joined by Weselmann in the shadows of the window.

"I wouldn't teach what Hitler's crowd wanted taught. For not following the party's guidelines, I was dismissed as a teacher and forced to enlist as a private. Only by the grace of God, I have survived five years of this war."

"I'm surprised they didn't throw you in a concentration camp for resisting the Nazis."

"You give me too much credit; at first, I believed in Hitler. I thought like the vast majority, he was good for Germany. The talk of the Jews was rhetoric, merely to form a united Germany. But actions followed the language, and being a coward, I did nothing. The few who did were either sent to concentration camps or executed. I didn't resist them, merely offended them," Weselmann replied in a somber tone.

"Then for God's sake, give it up after this fight. Don't keep making the same mistake of fighting for Hitler's gang. Germany will need men like you and Vopel to rebuild, instead of the Hitler clones like Gerickman," the American responded in an angry, pleading tone.

"Surrender? You know I can't."

"You and your—," stopping in mid-sentence, he motioned Weselmann to wake the two sleeping men before continuing,

"There's movement down there. Looks like dust being kicked up by several vehicles. Baumann, you awake?"

"Yes, Lieutenant," he replied with a yawn, rubbing his eyes.

"Signal Rickett and Vopel, possible vehicles advancing."

The soldier leaned out the window, giving hand signals to the non-coms.

"Lieutenant, Sergeant Rickett acknowledged the signal, but I don't know about the German corporal."

"Don't worry, Hans got the message. He doesn't want to reveal his position, in case some of Gerickman's men are close enough to view the village," Weselmann replied.

"Baumann, tell Baake here that we are holding this church and the old foundation, no retreat. Above all try and knockout the half-track. Sergeant Weselmann, Stempel and myself are holding the sanctuary. Good luck."

Glancing out the window, Baumann replied, "More dust kicking up, they're on their way."

"Let's go, Sergeant." Wallace ordered.

Running down the stairs, they were greeted by Perry and Piontek, both obviously in pain.

"What the hell do you two think your doing?" Wallace asked.

"We want to fight, Lieutenant," Perry said, acting as a spokesman for the two soldiers.

"Both of you get in that basement, that's an order. Doc, come up here and take care of these two." Waiting until Stazinski and the disappointed soldiers disappeared down the steps, he smiled continuing, "You realize that after this is over, neither of us can tell our superiors what we've done here?"

"I know. We would both be court-martialed and shot. I believe the charge would be aiding and abetting the enemy," Weselmann replied, moving a statue of St. Joseph away from the center window.

"Right, we'll just wait and tell the grand kids."

An excited Baumann raced down the stairs, blurting, "They'll be here in five minutes. By the size of the dust cloud, could be half a dozen vehicles or more."

"Ok, get back up there. Hold your fire until we open up, and stay out of sight."

Turning back to the window, he unclipped the grenades off his jacket, setting them in easy reach on the window's ledge. Checking the MP40, he nervously double-checked the safety. Glancing to his left, he grinned at Weselmann. Two days ago, this was his enemy. Today, he would fight and possibly die to save his life. Life is strange he thought, as the first of Gerickman's men began to emerge from the woods.

Chapter 20

As he held his breath, Wallace waited for the moment when as many of Gerickman's men as possible would be easy targets. Three truckloads of Gestapo quickly spread out at the edge of the woods, waiting for their opponents to give away their positions. The American lieutenant counted about twenty-five SS men warily edging closer to the church, taking cover every few steps until they were about thirty yards from the church. He hoped his men would hold their fire until the enemy entered the killing zone.

Vopel's group, occupying the houses across from the church, was holding its fire waiting for Wallace's signal. To Wallace's horror, he saw a squad of SS men emerge out of the north woods, stealthily moving to take the German corporal's position from the rear.

"Weselmann, do you see them?" Wallace whispered, pointing towards the houses across the road.

"Yes, I hope Hans posted someone to watch the north," he replied, concerned with the situation.

The Gestapo officer convinced no one had seen them, ordered a quick advance towards the houses. Weselmann's concern was unfounded as the enemy was greeted by heavy firing coming from the backside of the houses. Several SS men slumped to the ground, twitching momentarily before lying still. The rest, lead by a junior officer, went to ground to return fire, but after taking a few more casualties, including the officer, they panicked. The remainder jumped up, running back into the woods, but not before losing two more men.

Evidently the repulsed assault was Gerickman's signal to attack as firing erupted on the hilltop behind the church. The SS troopers at the west road poured fire into the houses, as they advanced on the first house, throwing in potato masher grenades through the windows. After the grenades went off, a small group rushed in through the doorway. Finding no occupants, they made ready to attack the next house; their biggest mistake was ignoring the church. They edged close enough to throw grenades at the second house when Wallace yelled, "Open fire!"

Caught in a vicious crossfire, the SS men assaulting the second house were reduced to bloody corpses, as the majority of the attacking force tried to turn left behind the church, moving through the garden. Weselmann moved quickly to a window on the opposite side of the church to cover the garden. Molotov cocktails, thrown from the steeple, burst in the midst of the advancing Gestapo, igniting the clothing of several men. Writhing on the ground, Weselmann ended their suffering with several bursts from his MP40. The rest fell back to the shelter of the trucks, unwilling to advance through another barrage of gasoline-filled wine bottles.

Out of effective rifle range and partially shielded by the trucks, two MG 42 heavy machine guns were hurriedly set up by their crews. They began a methodical raking of the houses and the church, spitting their deadly rounds. Pieces of wood and stone chipped away, slowly demolishing the houses and the church. The men in the houses and church were forced away from their firing positions.

"At the rate those weapons are tearing apart the houses, Vopel is not going to be able to hold out much longer," Wallace yelled, hunkering down away from the window, as an occasional round screamed through the opening.

"We've got to stop those guns, I'm going to the steeple," Weselmann shouted, not waiting for an order.

Bounding the stairs two at a time, he found the two men preparing more gasoline bombs.

"Never mind those. I have need of your special talent, Karl. Those two machine guns are a thorn in our plans, Do you have your telescopic sights?"

"Yes, Sergeant."

"Can you take out the gun crews from here?"

Peering over the edge Baake noticed only the heads of the gunners were visible, as he replied, "I don't know if I can hit the entire crew, but I can make them nervous."

"Good, make them nervous, Karl."

Weselmann watched as Baake produced a leather case containing the rifle sights. With a small screwdriver, he carefully attached the sights hoping they didn't need to be adjusted.

"Hurry Karl, I don't know how long Hans can hold those houses," Weselmann pleaded.

"I'm ready, Sergeant."

"Take out the gun on the right. It's doing the most damage."

Baake raised the gun over the edge of the steeple, adjusted the eyepiece, until the helmet of the gunner came into focus. Aiming just below the rim of the helmet, he slowly squeezed the trigger. The Mauser bucked against his shoulder, followed by a look of total unbelief on the face of the gunner as a trickle of blood leaked from his forehead. He slumped against his assistant who took his place until Baake's second round hit the man in the right eye spinning him away from the gun. There were no more takers for the dead men's position. Turning to the second machine gun, two well-placed rounds discouraged the remaining members of the gun crews.

Realizing where the deadly fire was coming from, the Gestapo hit the steeple with as much firepower as they could muster. The rounds smacked and zinged like a hive of angry bees, driving the three men to the floor of the steeple.

"Appears that you ticked them off pretty good," Baumann said.

"Good work, keep your heads down," Weselmann said, crawling to the staircase. "Mix up some more of those Russian cocktails as soon as the firing settles down. Remember your main target is the half-track."

Hurrying down the stairs, he thought, Gerickman's committed only half of his men. Where are the rest and the half-track?

Reaching the sanctuary he noticed Stempel and Wallace were back at the windows trying to pick off a careless SS man here and there. Moving to the vacant window, he was relieved to see three Mausers and a MP40 firing from the houses on the outside of the road. Evidently the torrent of MG42 rounds had not killed any of his men. The volume of firing decreased as the Gestapo were apparently pulling back to regroup.

"If Gerickman keeps hitting us like this, we should be all right. He's lost another thirty men. Either he's shot his bolt or he'll hit us with everything he's got left in the next round," summarized Wallace, sitting down on a pew near his window.

Stempel moved to the window vacated by the American lieutenant as he continued watching for any advance on the part of the Gestapo. The old, gray-haired soldier had been lucky. He removed his helmet pointing to the new crease, from a random machine gun round, in the cloth covering of his helmet, which brought a grin from Weselmann.

"You better tell him to get that pot back on his head before the next one parts more than his hair," Wallace said.

"*Fritz, bekommen diesen Sturzhelm auf Ihren Kopf, Ihr Sorgen Ihres amerikanischen Freunds zurüc.*"

Wallace watched the old man replace the helmet, noting that he was too old to be in a young man's war. Germany's army was deteriorating due to a lack of qualified replacements, but unfortunately not fast enough. Too many good units, made up of tough, veteran panzer grenadiers like these, will keep the war going. He admired their loyalty to their comrades, but in the end it was his duty to be a weapon of their demise. He shrugged off those thoughts for the moment. "I'm going to check the rest of the guys. Stay here, no need of both of us moving around."

Weselmann nodded in approval, returning to his window. The stress of the last two days was beginning to show in his face. Not only the responsibility of command but the new complexity of his personal life was weighing heavily upon him.

Outside the carnage wrought by the mixed force was more evident. Looking at the fallen SS, he thought that perhaps their private war was over. Gerickman had lost too many and didn't have enough left to attack with any hope of success. Any idea that it was over was shattered by the first mortar blast that landed 25 yards from the first house.

With the next blast, Wallace dove in the midst of Rickett's men, losing his helmet as he yelled, "Where did he get mortars?"

"Must have found a supply truck. Maybe, it was headed for the roadblock behind us," Rickett replied, as the next round landed in the church garden.

"The way those rounds are coming in, he doesn't have anybody that knows how to use one," Wallace said, peering over the edge of the foundation.

"Yeah, but even a bad mortar crew can get lucky, Lieutenant," Goldstein remarked, which proved to be a prophetic statement as the next round was a direct hit on the unattended jeep near the church cemetery.

"Goldstein, get over to the second house and tell Vopel to pull his men back to this position."

"Right, send the kid to get his tail shot off," he replied under his breath.

"You say anything, Goldstein?" Rickett asked not pleased with Goldstein's comments.

"Not really, I keep forgetting I volunteered for this assignment," he replied with a shrug of his shoulders.

"Then get your tail over there before I shoot it off myself. You heard the Lieutenant. Move it, soldier!" Rickett yelled.

The young infantryman, after sliding over the lip of the foundation, hesitated briefly before jumping to his feet and crossing the open space to the house. Disappearing inside, he reemerged with Vopel and his men in tow.

A mortar round hit very close to the trucks that were blocking the east road. Several figures scrambled away from the trucks like a scattered bunch of rabbits, melting into the woods.

"The way he's using that mortar, he may be more dangerous to his own men than us," Rickett mused, glancing a look towards his lieutenant. "You look worried. That mortar bothering you?"

"No, but what I'm worried about is what else does he have," Wallace replied, firing a couple rounds at some movement near the trucks. "Gerickman's smarter than I thought, attacked us to draw fire to locate our strong points. We need to reorganize our defense."

Goldstein and his companions jumped in the fortification alongside Wallace. A quick glance at the men revealed that they were no worse the wear from their ordeal, with the exception of some minor scrapes and bruises.

"I wonder how he got mortars?" Vopel asked.

"Corporal Vopel, then I take it, it's not standard issue for Gestapo troops," said Wallace.

"No, must have intercepted a munitions truck heading for Hauptmann Dietz's position. And that's not good."

"Why, what else could he have?" asked Wallace, hoping it was only ammunition but already knowing it was probably more trouble heading his way.

"All depends what was available in the supply dump and what Hauptmann Dietz called for. Could be panzerfausts, grenades, flamethrowers, ammunition—"

"That's enough, Corporal. I get the picture." The look on his face was grim and somber. "Any ideas, Jerry?"

"Attack."

"Sarge, are you nuts? That kraut has sixty or seventy men plus all that extra hardware." Goldstein exclaimed. "It's suicide."

"Settle down, Goldstein. I didn't have a frontal assault in mind," Rickett replied.

"Sergeant Rickett, I must agree with this youngster. To attack with our small force is rather reckless," Vopel said.

"Goldstein and Vopel are right, we only have thirteen men able to fight, an attack is out of the question," Wallace replied, shifting his position to get a better view of the road. His demeanor changed as a shrill whistle headed their way. "Down!"

The mortar round landed close to their position, showering the group with steel fragments. A cry of pain escaped the lips of Private Jenkins as a piece of the Krupp steel found his ribs, ripping through his combat jacket.

"Goldstein, get Doc here quick," Wallace shouted.

"Right, Lieutenant." said Goldstein, not hesitating at all; a friend's life could be at stake.

Jenkins held his hand against the wound hoping to stem the flow of blood. The look of sheer panic gripped his eyes as his sergeant asked him, "Let me take a look at that, kid."

"Sarge, I could bleed to death if I move my hands."

"It'll be all right. Let me look at it," Rickett said.

Rickett reached down carefully pulling up the wounded soldier's shirt to reveal a small, bleeding scratch. He looked at Wallace with a big grin. "Not quite a million-dollar wound is it, Lieutenant."

A relieved Wallace merely smiled at the embarrassed soldier who pulled away from Rickett. He quickly tucked in his shirt, trying to ignore the situation, knowing there were several who found the incident amusing. All was forgotten quickly as another round landed twenty-five yards left of their location.

"Lieutenant, we've got do something. Sooner or later he's going to drop one down our throats. And we're down to enough ammo to stop one more assault," said Rickett.

"I know, what's your plan?"

"Back in the States before the war I saw a Gary Cooper picture show about the Foreign Legion."

"What's that got to do with anything, Sarge?" Jenkins asked a definite edge to his voice.

"Give him a chance, Private. Go on, Sergeant," said Wallace.

"Like I said I saw this movie. In this movie to fool the Arabs attacking the fort, they propped up dead legionnaires to give the enemy the appearance that more men were still alive to defend the place when in reality only a few survived.

"None of our guys are dead. Where are we going to get dead Americans?"

Rickett pointed his thumb over his right shoulder. "We have plenty of dead Gestapo in that ravine. Slap an American helmet and jacket on a Gestapo corpse and from this distance they'll look like live soldiers. Gerickman won't be able to see what's going on because the ravine can't be seen from the east road because the church is in the way and the ground dips down."

"What about the Gestapo? Won't they be suspicious when nobody shoots back from here and the church?" Wallace asked.

"We leave four or five men in the town to fire from various locations. With all the dust that mortar is kicking up, it'll be hard to tell who is firing. That leaves enough of us to flank that mortar and knock out any other weapons he might have.

The medic and Weselmann exited the church doors and headed for Wallace's location. Running across the open ground, they drew an occasional rifle shot that smacked the ground near their feet. Stazinski reached the foundation ahead of the German sergeant who stopped to fire a short burst from his MP40 towards the trucks parked at the far end. Seeing the medic had reached safety, he swiftly resumed his pace until he jumped into the position.

The embarrassment revisited Jenkins as he exposed his minor misery to the medic who merely gave a slight smile before applying some sulfur and a bandage to the wound.

After watching Stazinski tend to Jenkins, Wallace turned back to Rickett. "What if Gerickman attacks before we hit him?"

"Well, Lieutenant, I think you already know the answer. It's a risk, the guys left in town could be overrun," the sergeant replied in a serious tone.

"What of the wounded and Sister Monique, they won't have a chance if the church is overrun? Herr Gerickman is not likely to take any prisoners," stated a concerned Weselmann.

"I doubt if Gerickman would venture out into the woods. I'll have Stazinski move the wounded a safe distance in the south woods. The nun can help with the wounded," Wallace replied, his answer seeming to relieve the German sergeant's concern.

"I'll help your medic with the wounded," said Weselmann, giving Wallace a nod before trotting off to the church. His real concern was to make the stubborn young woman not give reasons to stay behind. He was determined her safety was more important than any reason she might have not to leave.

"I won't order the men to stay as decoys. I want volunteers," said Wallace.

"Peter and I will stay behind." Vopel said after explaining the plans to his men.

"Count me in, Lieutenant," said Jenkins, not really sure why, but he was volunteering.

"It's my plan, I'm staying, Lieutenant. If anything goes wrong, I don't want anybody else to get killed," Rickett said.

"All of you remember I don't want dead heroes, if things get too hot, pull back to the woods. OK, let's get it done."

The men began the grisly task of retrieving the slain Gestapo bodies from the ravine. Wallace's men replaced the black helmets and tunics of the Third Reich with their own GI helmets and jackets. After selecting a Gestapo helmet, they decided due to the heat of the day, they didn't need to wear the blood-splattered tunics. Most were content to wear only their olive drab undershirts.

The so-called reinforcements were set up in the old foundation and the windows in the church, with empty weapons propped in their hands. From different views in the village, they looked alive and ready. It was only at a close inspection, could you see the expressionless faces and dead eyes of the lifeless figures.

But the worst dilemma for the men who stayed behind was the foul stench of death emanating from the Gestapo corpses. The soldiers, who volunteered, tied handkerchiefs over their mouths and noses in a vain effort to block the disgusting odor.

Running to the church, Wallace dove to the ground as a mortar round landed fifteen yards away, pelting him with debris. Picking himself up, he crossed to the building. When he arrived, Weselmann and Baumann opened the church door, allowing him inside.

"Well Sergeant, were you successful in getting Sister to leave with the wounded?" Wallace asked knowing his concern for her.

"They don't need to leave. They have a method of escape. She showed me a secret passage that leads from the back wall of the church basement to the south woods. She thinks it dates back to the French Revolution.

"Good, let's hope they don't need it."

"Lieutenant, you want me to stay here or go with you?" asked Baumann.

"What about your man in the steeple?"

"He knows the risk. He wants to stay," Weselmann replied.

"All right, Baumann you can go with us. First, go up and tell Baake to secure these doors."

Outside the raiding party gathered in a blind spot behind the church. Wallace, Weselmann, and six others, donned their German helmets while passing out the remaining grenades of which only five were left. All were armed with either MP40s or Mausers; most of the American weapons were without ammunition.

"By the trajectory of the rounds, the mortar is close to the road but whether on the south or north side, I don't know. Once we've located the mortar, we split up into two groups. Goldstein, Baumann, and Lepper, you three make up the first group. Sergeant Weselmann and his men will go with me."

"Why we splitting up, Lieutenant? We can do more damage together," Goldstein insisted working the bolt of the Mauser.

"Our main mission is to destroy the mortar and the supply truck. My group will hit the targets with grenades then fall back while Lepper's group gives covering fire to any pursuing Gestapo men."

A mortar round hit the side of the church without causing any damage, only leaving a billowing puff of smoke. A second round hit the garden helping to cloud any movement.

"OK, let's move. Either he's getting ready to attack or the mortar team doesn't have a clue they're firing smoke rounds. We'll follow the base of the hilltop through the garden, we can use the smoke for cover," Wallace said, quickly moving towards the woods behind the church.

The rest followed Wallace into the woods. With enough ammunition for one attack they had to succeed or die.

Chapter 21

The joy of the moment was not lost on Hauptmann Dietz's as Hauser's main body arrived. The German force at the roadblock swelled to over a hundred men with plenty of rations and ammunition. Overcome with emotion, several panzer grenadiers wept as they found lost friends in 3rd Company. Even the usually calm Dietz was moved to emotion as Hauser himself emerged from the woods. He looked bad, but Dietz hadn't seen a better sight in days.

"Thank God, you made it, Kurt. We were about out of ammunition and ready to pull out," Dietz said elatedly as he firmly clasped Hauser's hand and shoulder.

"You shouldn't have waited. We might all be cut off. The Americans have broken through everywhere. Have you seen any of my 2nd Platoon?" Hauser said.

"Only a corporal from your company named Weber."

"He's from 3rd Platoon. Anyone else?"

"No, except for a SS unit in the next village, we haven't heard of any other German units. Who is the officer in command of your platoon?"

"Lieutenant Liebig."

"I don't think I know him."

"He was a staff officer with Division headquarters."

"Any combat experience?"

"No, but I left him with one of my best sergeants, Weselmann."

"I'm afraid we can't wait for them," Dietz said, pulling out a pack of cigarettes then offering one to Hauser, "As soon as we can organize a withdrawal, I'm falling back."

"But what are you doing here? I thought your company was to dig in at the crossroads and hold," replied Hauser, following Dietz into his dugout.

"American Jabos shot up the column, that fool of a battalion commander had us moving on the road in daylight. Well, he already paid for his foolishness."

"When will they learn staff officers do not make good combat commanders," Hauser said, shaking his head.

"He was assured by higher command that we had air superiority in our sector. When was the last time we had command of the air?" Dietz mocked.

"I know the type. He wouldn't take any of your suggestions."

"I told him it was suicide to travel during the day, but the nephew of General von Martz knew better. Well enough of him, can your men be ready to move in fifteen minutes?"

"They're worn out but the need to get to our lines will keep driving them. You said there is an SS unit in the village. Any chance of transport?" asked Hauser.

"No, I asked if they could spare a truck for my wounded. Strumbannführer Gerickman said he could not spare any vehicles. The wounded would have to stay and die for the Führer, a noble sacrifice," an incredulous Dietz said, scanning the terrain in the direction of the road to the west with his binoculars.

"A noble sacrifice? There is nothing noble about seeing your men slaughtered," an angry Hauser replied. "In five years of this war, I can't remember seeing any Gestapo unit stay and fight. According to them, it's our duty to fight and die while they run and hide. All they are good for is slaughtering civilians."

"Before our radio went dead yesterday, I called for ammunition and rations, but the supply trucks must have been destroyed or captured.

Dietz continued to view the killing zone, littered with broken armored vehicles and corpses. Their protective cover was about gone, shattered by the routine artillery barrages and multiple aerial assaults. They had been lucky. Casualties were light from the support weapons, the majority of the deadly onslaught falling off target, but the American infantry had taken its toll.

"The majority of my men are spent. Can you assign a rearguard to cover the withdrawal?" Dietz asked, hating to give the responsibility to another.

"You risked your command to save mine. I will stay behind with my 1st Platoon to cover the retreat," Hauser replied.

"Give us an hour head start to get our wounded out, then fall back." Looking at his watch he said, "The Americans should hit you with an artillery barrage in the next fifteen minutes, followed by an armored assault. Their armor will be forced to follow the road where there are still a few anti-tank mines left. Expect flanking attacks from the infantry while their tanks hit the roadblock. Good luck, Kurt," Dietz said, extending his hand to his friend, hoping this wasn't the last time they would meet.

"I suggest you leave before the barrage begins. Don't worry we'll make it back." Hauser said, shaking his friend's hand.

"Krueger!" shouted Dietz.

"Yes, Herr Hauptmann."

"Gather the wounded. We are pulling out. Hauptmann Hauser's men will cover the retreat," Dietz said, stepping out of his dugout. He turned briefly to salute Hauser. "Goodbye my friend."

Twenty minutes had elapsed since Dietz's departure when the artillery opened up. The rounds screamed in a seemingly unrelenting fashion, more intense than any previous barrage. The area was blanketed by smoke and dust as screams of anguish rose from Hauser's position. The noise was deafening as one panzer grenadier went mad as he jumped and ran towards the American lines. Then after a few minutes of calm, there came the crackle of small arms fire intermingled with the squealing sound of tank tracks.

As the smoke and dust cleared, Hauser watched in horror as a M4 Sherman tank lumbered directly towards his position. A MG34 to his left opened up, its rounds bouncing harmlessly off the sides of the armored beast. A member of the machine gun crew fired a panzerfaust round that missed the tank and exploded harmlessly in the woods. The tank's turret rotated towards the threat, spewing a sheet of flame engulfing the crew. Satisfied the gun was no longer a threat, the turret swung back towards Hauser.

"*Flammespritzring!*" yelled several panicky voices, as the tank continued its trek towards Hauser. Rolling over one of the few remaining anti-tank mines, the tank came to an abrupt stop, smoke escaping from the view ports. For a moment or two nothing happened then the tank erupted, spewing flame from blown hatches. The force of the explosion knocked the turret askew. Somehow a lone, surviving crewman exited the vehicle his clothes in flames. A burst from the machine gun, on the right, ended his suffering.

Another American tank started to nudge the burning vehicle out of the way when a panzerfaust struck the front bogie wheel, disabling the left track. Its crew baled out, reaching the safety of the woods.

The concentrated fire of Hauser's remaining MG42 held back the American infantry advancing on his right flank until several grenades destroyed the gun. Without the support of the two flanking machine guns the position was doomed. The combat-seasoned veterans were overcome with panic, as additional armored vehicles appeared on the scene. In mass they attempted to head for the rear as accurate American fire reduced their number.

Hauser tried to stem the rout, yelling, "Hold your ground!" The stunned commander watched his 1st Platoon crumble before his eyes as he called familiar names, brave men he had known since the war began, but in vain. They all broke and ran like first-day recruits.

Dropping his Mauser rifle, he lowered his head into his hands in total despair, when he heard unfamiliar voices around him. Looking up, from his dugout, he stared into the barrels of several Thompson submachine guns.

"*Hande Hoch.*"

Realizing his war was over, he slowly raised his hands.

"Kowalski, tell Captain Neilson we got us a kraut officer."

"Yeah, maybe he can tell us what happened to Lieutenant Wallace and the guys, Sarge."

Rusty Cooper held his weapon on Hauser, eyeing the decoration around the German officer's neck. Thinking it would make a nice addition to his collection of Nazi souvenirs, he reached his hand out to grab the Iron Cross, which the proud Hauser pushed away.

"All right kraut, dead or alive, I don't care," he said, pointing his weapon at Hauser's head. "I want that medal."

"Hold it, Cooper. I need this officer alive," said Captain Neilson, arriving in time to save the unbowed German.

"But Captain don't I get a bonus for capturing an officer?"

"After I get the information on the whereabouts of Jack Wallace's unit, you can have his medals and anything else he has." Neilson looked down at the German officer's belt. "I would start with his sidearm. How long have you been in the Army? Didn't they teach you anything in boot camp?"

"May I put my hands down? I will gladly give your sergeant my pistol," said Hauser, annoyed with the Americans' conversation.

The American captain nodded to his German counterpart, who undid the flap of his holster and handed the pistol to Cooper.

"Good, you speak English. That will make things easier," Neilson replied.

"Hauptmann Kurt Hauser, W0983456789."

"Sit down, Herr Hauptmann. I want some information on my missing patrol from two days ago."

"According to the Geneva Convention, I do not need to say anything other than what I have already told you. I expect proper attention, according to my rank. But to refresh your mind, Hauptmann Kurt Hauser, W0983456789."

Neilson's eyes narrowed, as he stared at the arrogant German officer.

"Herr Hauptmann," Neilson's tone became more sinister, "you will answer my questions or suffer the fate of your men. One more dead kraut will hardly be noticed. We found one of our jeeps at the clearing off the main road. What happened to my men?"

Hauser looked away from Neilson to scan the death and destruction wrought by the two sides as a good half of his men laid dead or badly wounded. A sense of guilt rose within him, that he survived when others did not.

Turning back to Neilson, he said, "I know nothing of your men. We reinforced the unit that held the roadblock. They might know what happened to your patrol."

"Where are they now, the other unit?"

"That I will not tell you. Kill me if you wish, but I will not be the cause of more deaths."

"Cooper."

"Yes, Captain."

"Get transport to take Hauptmann Hauser to headquarters for further questioning."

"Right, sir."

"Cooper, let the man keep his medals."

A disappointed Cooper organized a small group of soldiers to take Hauser and half a dozen other prisoners to the American intelligence officers. Before leaving Hauser gave his counterpart a salute which was ignored by Neilson.

"Kowalski, how long before the road is clear enough to get vehicles up the road."

"Hour or two, Captain. Those last knocked out tanks have the road blocked pretty good."

"Tell Lieutenant Hodgins, I want him. This trench is the temporary Company CP."

Taking a drink from his canteen, he thought if he had given Wallace a platoon instead of a squad and a few armored vehicles, he wouldn't have the problem of locating his lost patrol. He hadn't found any bodies, so maybe they are just holed up somewhere. He was sure the answer was in the next village.

Chapter 22

Back in Nueviant, a small probing attack was being beaten back by accurate small arms fire. Wallace could hear the heavy firing of his only machine gun spitting its final rounds before running out of ammunition. Without covering fire from the hilltop, there would be little chance for the men in the village to hold back Gerickman's next attack unless their mission succeeded. Their pace would have to speed up, throwing caution aside, as Gerickman's support weapons had to be destroyed.

"Sounds like the boys beat them back, Lieutenant," Goldstein whispered. "I don't hear any more firing."

Raising his voice slightly, without breaking the pace, he sternly replied to the young soldier, "Hold it down, Goldstein. I don't think any of them spotted us, so let's keep the advantage."

The section of woods was filled with briar bushes which made their trek more difficult but also assured that few Gestapo men would be present. The thorns shredded their uniforms, welting their bodies, but the disciplined troops made no sound.

To confirm Wallace's earlier statement the soldier on point, Corporal Lepper, who was about ten yards ahead, suddenly froze. He slowly turned signaling Wallace and Weselmann to join him.

To their right, small groups of SS men were standing near the road, evidently expecting an order to advance. Twenty yards behind them was the remaining half-track, with a full complement of Gestapo riders. By their appearance and demeanor the next attack could come at any time.

The faint sounds of the mortar were barely audible from their present position. They all gauged that its location was on the other side of the road, shielded by the majority of the Gestapo unit. The situation was not good.

"I don't like it, Lieutenant," Lepper whispered. "If we hit that mortar, we'll be cut off with fifty or sixty angry krauts on our tails. We won't stand a chance."

Several moments of silence passed as Wallace and Weselmann scanned the Gestapo position, before the American lieutenant made his decision. Moving back to the main body, he explained his plan.

"Ok, this is what we are going to do. Sergeant Weselmann, I need a volunteer to take out that mortar. Want the job?"

Weselmann looked to the ground contemplating his options before nodding his agreement. He wanted to survive but if he sensed correctly what Wallace had in mind, his chances were slim, but it was the only way to get his men home.

"Good," Wallace said, acknowledging the German's intention.

"What's your plan, Lieutenant?" Lepper asked.

"Give your grenades to Weselmann. The two of us are going to circle around behind their position and toss in these eggs. Hopefully we can knock out the mortar and the supply truck if it's close to the mortar. When you hear the explosions open up on the road, cause as much confusion as you can. Fall back to the village as soon as they advance on your position."

"That's nuts, Lieutenant. You two will be cut off with a lot of Germans chasing after you," the baffled soldier whispered.

"I'm counting on your group to draw the majority of the Gestapo in your direction," said Wallace knowing the odds weren't good. "It's 10:37, give us fifteen minutes. If you don't hear these go off, head for home. Above all, don't wait for us."

Weselmann gathered his men to him, explaining the plan. By the looks and gestures they had the same reaction as the American corporal.

Wallace popped the magazine of his MP40, checking the rounds he had left. By his estimation only twenty-eight rounds remained. Not only were they running out of time but ammunition as well.

They moved parallel to the road, ever alert for hidden sentry posts. Fortunately, the security on the part of the SS was poor. Evidently it was beyond Gerickman's thinking that he would be attacked by so small a group of men, as a lone sentry patrolled on their side of the woods.

Private Rolf Rauser stood leaning against an old tree staring towards the road. He wondered, after all this, if Herr Gerickman would let him keep the motorcycle. He almost was out of this mess but Klinemann died before he could be transported to a field hospital. Rauser thought maybe a promotion to corporal was in order if Herr Gerickman was satisfied with his performance.

Continuing to watch the road, he seemed more concerned in being caught by one of his officers than any threat from another source. The SS man was taken totally by surprise as Weselmann emerged in front of him, apparently surrendering. Before Rauser could yell a warning, Wallace who had crept up behind him, quickly slipped his left hand over the man's mouth to stifle any scream, as the blade in his right hand plunged into soft muscle of the Gestapo man's heart. All surprise and any other thoughts faded as Rauser slumped to the forest floor.

After wiping his blade on the dead man's uniform, Wallace returned his knife to its scabbard. Weselmann slung the dropped Mauser after checking the clip. Wallace searched the body, finding an additional five round clip. Tossing the clip to his companion, they dragged the body to a depression in the ground and then covered it with some branches.

"I don't see anybody else. I guess this poor soul was the only sentry," Wallace whispered.

"Another twenty meters and we'll be behind them."

"Good, at that point the road bends. They shouldn't be able to spot us crossing to the other side."

As Wallace moved forward, Weselmann tugged at the lieutenant's sleeve. The American turned with a puzzled look expecting to see a new threat.

Glancing around and seeing no apparent threat he whispered, "What's the problem?"

"It's Sister Monique, I mean Michelle," he replied a touch of tenderness in his voice.

"Sergeant, we don't have time for this now. Gerickman could launch a major attack any time now. We have to knock out that mortar!" Wallace implored.

Ignoring the American for the moment, he replied, "I know she'll want to go with my men and me. I want you to take her to safety. She'll have a better chance to survive with you."

"Then, you two are in love."

"Yes, it wasn't the cause of all this, but it did play a part."

"Is she really a nun?"

"Yes, when I entered Nueviant she was prepared to take her final vows in a few months, but the circumstances of the last few days have changed that. I tried to talk her out of it, but I know she'll want to come with me. And that will be dangerous for her."

"I promise to get her out of the area, but right now we need to stop that mortar."

"I'm in your debt, Lieutenant," Weselmann gratefully replied, following the already moving Wallace.

Wallace checked his watch then pointed to a small clearing near the road. "We've got eleven minutes left. We better chance a crossing here."

Crawling to the edge of the road, they sprinted across after checking for any Gestapo in the immediate vicinity. Once on the north side, they found a narrow deer path that ran parallel to the dirt road. After a couple of minutes they found the mortar manned by three men. The supply truck was ten yards behind the crew, some of its cargo stacked in a random pile. Two SS men stood opening the crates, looking for any weapons that could be used against the defenders of Nueviant. A dozen gas cans had been stacked close to the side of the truck alongside several panzerfausts and three crates marked *handgranate*.

Checking their watches, they realized that they had four minutes left before attacking the mortar crew. As quietly as possible, they moved into grenade range of the conveniently stacked gas cans.

"Get ready. Throw a couple grenades into that pile of gas cans after I open up on the two men opening crates," whispered Wallace, who received a slight head nod from Weselmann. "After you toss those pineapples, run like hell. Don't worry about the mortar crew. Doesn't look like they have more than a few rounds left to fire."

A large group of SS men, walked towards the mortar crew, led by none other then Strumbannführer Kurt Gerickman. Whatever the reason for his arrival, it put a fair-sized unit in an excellent position for pursuit. They had run out of time.

Firing from the prone position, Wallace's first burst splintered wooden crates. It also caught one of the Germans in the chest as he slumped down out of sight. The other German ducked behind the crates and began returning fire from a newly acquired MP40. His mouth dropped open as he saw two grenades bounce among the gas cans. With wild eyes he attempted to flee before the grenades caused a tremendous explosion, engulfing the truck, the crates, and himself. The force of the explosion flung the SS man, his clothes afire, arcing like a roman candle towards the bewildered mortar crew. The sight of their comrade's death was too much for the panic stricken crew who broke and ran.

Wallace and Weselmann had taken refuge behind a huge oak, seconds before the grenades had ignited the gasoline. The burning truck, filled with crated ammunition, began spraying its deadly cargo in all directions.

Through the flames of the truck, Weselmann could see the utter confusion of the Gestapo troops as flanking fire erupted from Lepper's group stationed in the woods. Several vehicles parked alongside the road burst into flames as small arms fire found their gas tanks. Several SS men toppled from the half-track as the driver put the vehicle in full reverse. Finding a wide place in the road to turn around, it pulled up to a screaming Gerickman. As the remaining SS men disembarked, Herr Strumbannführer appeared to be in a violent conversation with the driver. The half-track then lurched forward picking up speed as Gerickman drew his pistol to fire some harmless rounds at the retreating vehicle.

"Looks like some of Herr Gerickman's men have had enough," Weselmann commented.

"Unfortunately he still has enough to give us problems," replied Wallace. "Let's get out of here."

A group of twenty men, led by Gerickman, ran towards Wallace and Weselmann. The pair fired a quick burst thinning the ranks of the pursuing unit, then headed back into the woods. Stopping every few feet, they fired random bursts behind them. Finally they reached a gully with fairly steep banks.

"I think we've run as far as we can go. Trying to climb out here makes us easy targets."

"How's your ammunition?" asked Wallace.

"Less than half a clip for the MP40, 9 rounds for the Mauser, and one grenade."

"About the same counting my .45 caliber and two grenades. That should be enough to get some of them."

"We'll find out pretty quick. Here they come!" Weselmann exclaimed, falling to the ground as Gerickman's lead troopers came into view.

The Gestapo took cover as two black-clad soldiers fell dead from a quick burst of Wallace's MP40. Three SS men tried to swing to the left but ran into the blast of Weselmann's lone grenade, killing all of them.

"Spread out," Gerickman yelled. "I want Weselmann alive."

Two of Gerickman's men were slow to react to his command and were rewarded with a grenade from Wallace, leaving their lifeless bodies strewn on the forest floor. Flinging his empty MP40 away, Weselmann used his newly acquired Mauser. With his MP40 empty, Wallace fired his .45 caliber sidearm ammo until it was gone as well. With their final rounds, the two trapped soldiers had whittled the attacking force down to seven men. Wallace's last grenade killed a single Gestapo man who foolishly tried rushing their position. Abruptly the deadening sounds of battle ceased.

"Advance!" Gerickman shouted, his men cautiously rising from cover.

Wallace and Weselmann waited for the inevitable. The remaining Gestapo closed on the doomed pair.

"Sorry, Lieutenant. I had wished a better end to our truce."

"No apologies necessary, Sergeant. It was a good try," he replied. His answer felt a little melodramatic, more appropriate for a B movie.

"At least Michelle will be all right. He doesn't have enough men left to attack the village."

"*Hande Hoch!*" Gerickman's men screamed.

The two defiant men tossed their empty weapons away. With raised hands, both men expected the sting of death. The SS men roughly shoved Wallace against the trunk of a big tree ready to end his life. Weselmann was left for the moment to the personal attention of their commander.

"Wait! I want this American swine to see what I am going to do with this traitor," Gerickman sneered. Unsheathing his SS dagger, he continued. "You will soon see what happens to the scum that crosses my path."

Three men trained their rifles on Wallace as Gerickman, with slow deliberate steps, moved closer to the panzer grenadier. Flanked on either side by a Gestapo man armed with a MP40, he stopped three feet in front of the defiant Weselmann. With a sinister look adorning his face, he fondled the SS dagger as he waved it menacingly near the Wehrmacht soldier's face.

"You have caused me a great deal of embarrassment, Weselmann. I can give a quick death, or you can linger in extreme pain. I guarantee you, that I know methods of slow death. Where are my valuables?" he whispered his lies. He had no intention of any quick death for the two men.

"Herr Strumbannführer, I am not a fool. Do you really believe that I can trust you? No matter what I say, you are planning to avenge that brother of yours. The rest of our men are safe from you and for that I thank God. Soon the American army will have your lost gold and jewels, and from that I get some small measure of pleasure," Weselmann grinned.

"Weselmann, before I finish with you, you will be cursing that God of yours. I'm going to enjoy this. Lohr, tie him to that tree."

Slinging his machine pistol, Lohr shoved Weselmann towards a sturdy tree a few feet away. Weselmann went to a knee, causing the Gestapo sergeant to think he accidently stumbled. His fall brought an outburst of laughter from Gerickman's men. Reaching down to pick up Weselmann, the laughing SS man's face changed quickly. Weselmann lunged upwards with the hidden knife from his boot, plunging it into Lohr's soft belly. The nimble sergeant shoved the screaming man towards his friends while pulling the MP40 off Lohr's shoulder. Before the slow reacting SS could fire, he fired a burst that killed two of the three men guarding Wallace.

The third man ignored the American lieutenant trying to shoot Weselmann. Wallace took advantage of the situation by kicking the man's leg as hard as he could. A loud snapping sound preceded the SS man falling in front of Wallace. Using the fallen man as cover, Wallace picked up the discarded rifle. The SS man writhed in pain on the ground until Gerickman's errant pistol shot fell short killing his own man. Wallace's aim was better as he killed the Gestapo man next to Gerickman with a shot through the heart. The Strumbannführer fired a second shot hitting Wallace in the arm, knocking him behind the big tree. It was Herr Gerickman's last conscious act as Weselmann's second burst stitched a neat pattern across the Black Heart's chest. Staring at the hated sergeant, he slumped to his knees before falling face down into a pile of brush, joining his brother in Hell.

Wallace, holding his arm, joined Weselmann sitting on a boulder near the fallen Gerickman.

"How bad is it?" Weselmann asked, tying a tourniquet around the lieutenant's arm.

"I'll live. Didn't hit the bone. Not much more than a flesh wound. Good thing Gerickman wasn't much of a marksman."

"What's next? Does this end our truce?"

"We can talk about that later. First, we gather our squads. They're scattered over this whole area," said Wallace.

Weselmann reached down and picked up the dagger and scabbard of the late Strumbannführer, handing it to Wallace.

"Here is something to remind you of our time together in the years to come," Weselmann smiled.

"Hopefully, both of us will have years left." A shot of pain hit his arm as he winced, "Let's get back before any of Gerickman's men come back."

Flinging away their Gestapo helmets, they walked down the road past the burning wreckage of trucks and staff cars. Many black-clad men were lying prone in the road or burning with their vehicles. They slowed briefly to checkout the dead Gestapo, unaware that a MP40 was being trained on their unsuspecting backs. Another hand appeared to lower the weapon.

"What are you doing, Heinz. I can kill them both."

"Let them go, Guenther. They have done us a great favor."

"What do mean? They're going to have Gerickman's staff car with all the gold and jewels."

"I had the opportunity to take a look in the trunk of that car. The valuables are gone. The sly devil must have hid them last night."

"But why let Weselmann get away with killing Herr Gerickman?"

"Simple, Guenther. Twenty of our men followed Gerickman into the woods after those two devils. You might miss. Why take the chance. With all the officers dead, only the three of us know where our beloved, dead commander could have hidden his share of the valuables."

"But we're not sure exactly where he went last night."

"Except a good guess would be the deserted village east of here."

"But what of Weselmann and his men. Do we allow them to get away with killing Herr Strumbannführer and his brother?"

"The Gerickmans. You want to give away a chance for riches because of them? They were stealing the Führer's treasure. Weselmann did the Third Reich a favor killing them."

"But the rest?"

"Mostly strangers. I didn't lose any close friends."

"But, what do we do?"

"We get to Strasbourg and report that Allied aircraft destroyed the column and the survivors were killed by partisans."

"Will they believe it?"

"Our columns are routinely shot to pieces. They'll believe it."

"Then after the war, we settle down in this part of France. Come on, let's get going."

Walking back to the waiting half-track, they found a wounded SS officer and two enlisted men.

"Mueller, turn your vehicle around. We must avenge our comrades."

"I don't think so," Mueller replied, firing from the hip as he mowed down the unsuspecting trio of men. "I have other plans."

Stepping over the dying men, he climbed aboard the half-track before heading towards Strasbourg.

"Aw hell, Heinz. Did you have to kill them?"

"Did you want them to tell what really happened here?

"They might have gone along with our plans."

"I already have two partners, I don't need anymore."

The lone half-track, all that remained of Gerickman's unit, sped down the road. A short distance away, west of the fleeing vehicle, Wallace and Weselmann heard the firing that killed the three SS men.

"You think some of our men came looking for us?" Weselmann asked.

"I hope not. Maybe it's partisans finishing off the remnants of the Gestapo. Just in case, we better make double time to the village in case we have to organize another rescue mission."

As they spoke small arms firing erupted from the west.

"It's not the village, but it sure sounds close."

"I can only assume the roadblock has fallen and our units are fighting," Weselmann replied.

Two trucks headed their way as they dove for cover. The lead truck stopped and a familiar voice yelled, "Lieutenant, we're pulling out."

"Jerry?"

"Come on, Lieutenant. Everybody is out of the village." Rickett responded tensely, tossing an American helmet and jacket to Wallace.

"Michelle?" Weselmann asked.

"She's in the other truck with Vopel and your men."

"All of our guys here?"

"Everybody's here! There's a full company of Germans occupying Nueviant. They could be heading this way. We've got to move, Lieutenant."

"What about Gerickman's men? Any left in Nueviant?"

"I don't think so, Lieutenant. I think we got them all."

"The cases with the valuables?"

"In our truck."

"All right, Jerry," he replied, turning to Weselmann. "I won't ask you to surrender. I know it wouldn't do any good. Our men did fight well together."

"I will miss you, Lieutenant."

"Good luck, Sergeant," said Wallace, shaking his enemy's hand. Hope I don't see you or any of your men until after this war is over."

"I wish the best for you and your men."

The young woman, dressed in simple peasant garb, climbed down from the second truck and ran to the German sergeant who embraced her in his arms and kissed her. He then lifted her up and placed her in the truck next to Wallace.

"Franz, what are you doing?"

"I will see you after this war is over. You will always be in my thoughts. Goodbye, Michelle."

"No, Franz" she pleaded. "You will be killed."

"You'll be safer with the Americans. Remember Michelle, God is with us always. He got all of us through the last two days. I believe it's His will that we will be together."

With that Weselmann snapped to attention, saluting the American lieutenant before turning away and running to the second truck. The truck slowly turned around and headed back to Nueviant.

"Don't worry, Michelle. He'll be okay. He's a survivor," Wallace said in a soothing voice.

Watching the truck disappear down the west road as tears swelled in her eyes, she replied, "I know."

Wallace leaned back against the bench seat of the truck staring in the direction of Nueviant. He had survived overwhelming odds. They had all survived. Were we really that lucky or was God on our side like Weselmann said? God, I hope I don't see that man or any of his men until this madness called war is over. Until then we still have a job to do.

"Jerry, let's get out of here and back in the war."

"Right, Lieutenant," he replied, tapping the back of the truck cab.

Goldstein, at the wheel, meshed the gears of the Opel truck and headed east for the safety of the American lines. The truck groaned with each shift of the lever as it slowly picked up speed. And then it disappeared as well.

The truce was over.